W9-BXS-924

NEW ALBANY-FLOYD COUNTY PUBLIC LIBRARY

ROMANCE   NOV 2 0 2002
Galloway, Shelley.
The love letter /
M   294219

WITHDRAWN

NEW ALBANY-FLOYD COUNTY PUBLIC LIBRARY
IN NEW BOOKS THRU JUL 2003

NEW ALBANY-FLOYD COUNTY PUBLIC LIBRARY

3 3110 00478 7014

THE LOVE LETTER

•

Shelley Galloway

AVALON BOOKS
NEW YORK

© Copyright 2002 by Shelley Galloway Sabga
Library of Congress Catalog Card Number: 2002092786
ISBN 0-8034-9567-6
All rights reserved.
All the characters in this book are fictitious,
and any resemblance to actual persons,
living or dead, is purely coincidental.
Published by Thomas Bouregya Co., Inc.
160 Madison Avenue, New York, NY 10016

PRINTED IN THE UNITED STATES OF AMERICA
ON ACID-FREE PAPER
BY HADDON CRAFTSMEN, BLOOMSBURG, PENNSYLVANIA

For my sister, Kelley.
Thank you for always being there for me.

Chapter One

*Please join me at 3:00 P.M. on Sunday for a picnic in
the park. The meal will be good, and the company, I
am certain, excellent.*

Fondly,
Me

Millicent Drovers read her invitation again with pleasure, then carefully folded and set it on her best friend
Chrissie's doorstep. Then, with a swish of her gray skirts,
she carefully made her way back down the walkway and
headed home.

As she thought again of her somewhat formal invitation,
she smiled to herself. While it was true that most people
did not care to write out invitations to friends they had
known since grade school, Millicent figured she and Chrissie were an exception to the rule.

Long ago they had decided that since theirs was a special
relationship, it deserved special treatment. Over the years,

they had formally invited each other to tea, to birthday celebrations, and to Sunday suppers.

Many would probably chide them if the notes were made known. People in Rocky River, Colorado, weren't known for putting on airs, or for suffering those who did. Rocky River was a hardworking town, the silver lode having made many prosperous beyond their wildest imaginings. People here were on the cusp of something special, and each person seemed aware of it.

Because, for goodness' sakes, no other town could boast of having close to twenty restaurants, an opera house, a dance hall, and a variety theater. Add being a focal point of the Gold Belt Rail Line, and folks couldn't be prouder of where they lived! However, knowing so didn't stop the awareness that each person put on their pants one leg at a time.

Of course, many would have also tended to agree that Millicent Drovers was rather special herself, even for as special a town as Rocky River. She carried a gleam in her eye, a bounce in her step, and a kind word for most folks.

Miss Millicent had lost her mother during their first winter in the city, her mother being of a fragile constitution. Her daddy had been killed in the mine shaft collapse of 1889, two years before. Since then, she made ends meet by living frugally off the money her father, Robert Drovers, had saved in the bank, and by taking in mending and sewing.

By some standards, she was considered an old maid at twenty-two. But she was exceptional. She had lovely wavy light brown hair and deep indigo eyes, so dark you would think they were brown if you didn't look hard enough. One person had even been heard saying that looking into Miss

Millicent's eyes was just like staring into a dark pool of water, looking both wondrous and deep.

Millicent was also praised because she didn't shun prospective suitors, either. They just had to wait their turn, was all. Millicent accepted invitations on Saturday evenings to the opera house, to the Spangler Variety Theater, or to a nice dinner at one of the many restaurants in town. If a man wanted to spend some time alone with her, why he just had to get a reservation, so to speak. Already, she was booked up through April. But rumor had it the end of May was looking good.

However, none of that crossed Millicent's mind as she walked home that evening. She thought only of the pile of mending needing to be done, a project for the church bazaar she was working on, and dinner to make. If she was sad to be dining by herself, or that the evening was sure not to have any spark at all, she kept it to herself.

Things were best that way.

Tucked neatly into her bed, she was unaware of the wind that came up that night. Her note was blown clear off of Chrissie's front stoop and flew two houses down to rest for a spell in the Herglesberger's front lawn. It was then carried across the dusty road to land at the corner of Mr. Smith's and Mr. Marshall Bond's homes. Early the next morning the ice cart ran over it.

An hour after that, Mr. Paulson, the dairy man, walked by, saw it, and feeling the Good Samaritan, took the letter up to Marshall's front step and secured it with a rock, assuming it belonged to the saloon owner.

And Marshall, on his way out two hours later, almost tripped over the thing. Thinking that it was yet another invoice or bill for the saloon, he pocketed it and made his way down the street.

It wasn't until he was at the Dark Horse Saloon, seated at one of the tables, visiting with his friend George, and sorting through his correspondence, that Marshall remembered the note.

George was currently expounding on his reasons for hiring Chrissie McKenna at the mercantile, the least of which was that he was in love with her. Since this was nothing new to hear, Marshall half listened as he unfolded the letter, read it, and then read it again.

"Hold on a sec, George," he said, staring at the paper in confusion.

The contents gave him a start. "What do you make of this?"

George read the note. "Woo-whee." He whistled under his breath. "Looks like you've got yourself a secret admirer."

The thought was disturbing. "I don't know about that."

George laid the paper flat on the table, smoothing out the creases. "Look at this writin', at that curly-cue on the 'P'. A female wrote this note for sure."

Marshall had to agree with George's assessment, but remained confused. "But why?" he asked. "Why would some lady decide to ask me to picnic confidentially?"

George merely shrugged.

Marshall continued. "After all, I know just about everyone in this town . . . and anybody who knows me realizes it's no hardship to ask me to do things . . . even if it is picnicking."

George looked at his friend in understanding. "True.

You've been to more church picnics and soirées than the average saloon owner, that's a fact."

Marshall thought back to the other outings he had been asked to attend just in the last month. Dinners, dances, and even one birthday party for an eighty-year-old spinster. Through it all, he had gone willingly. After all, that was his business of sorts—to get to know people. His saloon wasn't merely a drinking establishment, it was more like a gentlemen's club.

And good sense led him to believe that the best way to encourage business was to encourage relationships with the people of Rocky River. In order to do that, he attended more house parties and luncheons in town than he figured most of the society matrons did. Most everybody knew that. That's why a secret note just didn't make sense. He screwed up his face as he looked at the note again. "This seems different somehow."

George eyed the handwriting. "It does have an air of mystery to it."

"You could say that."

"Who do you think sent it?"

Marshall shrugged. "Don't know." There were roughly one thousand people in Rocky River at the present time, though he figured only about half could read. Out of that number, only a fourth were women, and only about a fourth of that were women who were single and of marriageable age.

As he skimmed through his mental list of women he had accompanied lately, he realized there were even fewer that would have the gumption to do something like this.

He had to admit it; the note was intriguing.

George leaned back on his chair, the two back legs creaking in response. "What are you going to do?"

"Don't know," Marshall said again. "Think about it for a while, I guess. Maybe nothing."

George leaned forward. The front legs of his chair tapped against the floor as he did so. "I wouldn't think too long," he said, pointing to the neat script. "You're supposed to picnic on Sunday, and it's already Wednesday."

"True."

"Now, Marshall, the thing is, you don't want just to go down to that picnic unprepared."

"I think you have a point, there."

"You ought to have an inklin' of who it would be who would be meeting you at the park. Who knows, it could be a plot to get you in a compromising position."

Marshall was catching on. Last thing he wanted to be doing in the spring was to attend his own shotgun wedding. He raised his eyes to George. "I think that maybe a little detective work is in order."

"Good idea. Now, what you need is a list of suspects." George nodded, serious as could be.

Marshall scowled at the word. "We're talking about women, not criminals."

George quirked an eyebrow. "There would be some who would say criminals and marriageable women are one and the same. It's all a matter of us not getting caught in their grasp."

Marshall grinned. "You may have a point there." And with that, he called to his best bargirl, Sadie, and asked her to bring him a pencil and some paper. It was time to make a list of women who would be interested in him. And although he didn't speak of it out loud, Marshall could humbly say that the list was bound to be rather long, indeed.

Chapter Two

"Oh, dear," Millicent said when Chrissie told her that she had never received her invitation. "I distinctly recall setting it right on your doorstep last night, under a light-colored rock."

"Well, the wind was fierce last night. I guess it blew away."

"I wonder where to?"

Chrissie looked at her friend with interest. "Does it matter?"

"I guess not," Millicent admitted as she leaned back in the rocking chair with a sigh. "It's just the thought that my personal note is, as we speak, floating through our town . . . it just doesn't sit right with me, is all."

"All you should be thinking about is what I should wear to dinner with you this Saturday. Who is taking you out again?"

"I'm not sure," Millicent said honestly. "I'll have to look at my calendar."

Chrissie laughed at her friend's earnest expression. "Don't you ever look forward to these outings? You always look so vague when you speak of them."

"I don't mean to be, they just seem to run together."

"You need to pick someone who interests you, like I did with George, and go out with him more than once," Chrissie said with an air of certainty. "It's time to give some of these men a chance."

"Perhaps. I don't know." Millicent shrugged, then rocked back again. She couldn't help feeling restless. It was as if her life was on hold, just waiting for something to happen; anything to shake things up.

"So, what do you think?" Chrissie prodded. "My blue gingham or the periwinkle with the lace collar?"

"Definitely the periwinkle. It brings out the color of your eyes, I think."

They rocked some more in silence, Millicent lost in her thoughts as she speculated; Chrissie thinking about her wardrobe. Then they were interrupted by the arrival of George himself. He had just come up on the sidewalk and was bearing a trout wrapped in newspaper.

He tipped his hat as he climbed the four steps to Chrissie's front porch. "Miss Chrissie, Miss Millicent."

Millicent nodded in response. "Hello, George."

Happily, Chrissie stood as he approached. "George, you brought me a fish?"

He grinned. "I got lucky this afternoon and knew you and your pa would appreciate it."

Chrissie stepped forward and accepted his gift, holding the well-wrapped fish at arm's length. "Hold on a minute; let me go put this in the sink. Have a seat, George, will you?"

"I've got a few minutes. Thank you, Chrissie."

Millicent eyed George with amusement as his eyes followed Chrissie's steps into the house. There weren't too many men who could deliver a fish with such finesse. "Now who said a way to a woman's heart was flowers?" she teased.

George chuckled. "Whoever said that didn't know Chrissie. She's a woman who can appreciate a four-pound trout."

"She is a fine cook. Now I, on the other hand, would fry the poor thing to a crisp!"

"Perhaps that is why I didn't bring a fish for you," he retorted.

Millicent laughed, enjoying their conversation. She had known George since the time when she used to go fishing, too, and over the years they had developed a healthy camaraderie. He was surely the brother she had never had.

Leaning back, she once again admired his short red hair, blue eyes, and easy disposition. He was handsome and amusing, and had a kindness that all who knew him appreciated. Chrissie was justifiably lucky to have him for a beau. "How was your day? Are things busy at the mercantile?"

George shrugged. "Fair to middlin'. It was quiet enough that I sat for a spell with Marshall at the Dark Horse."

Millicent pressed a hand to her chest to calm the flutter she felt at hearing Marshall's name. "How is he?"

George looked at her speculatively. "He's fine, I guess."

Sorry for no more information, Millicent tried to make her voice sound carefree. "I'm pleased to hear that."

George waited another beat or two, then seemed to take pity on her. "He's had an interesting day, I reckon."

"Oh, really?" she asked, as she reluctantly admitted to

herself that she just couldn't help but be interested. After all, there was just something about Marshall that she couldn't help but admire. Perhaps it was those dark eyes, always so alert, so quick to notice details. Or, maybe it was that slick black hair that drew her . . . so shiny, just like an otter's . . . or his strong jaw? She pursed her lips. Maybe it was the fact that he was one of the few men in town who had never asked her out for a Saturday night date.

Though they'd been friends almost as long as herself and George, she was sorry that Marshall had never been eager to turn the corner where their friendship was concerned. He seemed to be perpetually happy that they were friends and nothing more. Although there was that time when they'd waltzed during Peggy Sue Johnston's wedding two years ago.

Bringing herself back to the present, she asked, "What happened?"

"He's got himself a secret admirer."

She inhaled sharply. Of all the things George could have said, that was not one she expected. "Why would you say that?"

"He found a letter on his stoop this morning."

A strong sense of foreboding filled her heart. "A letter?"

George grinned. "An offer to a picnic, actually. Sunday." George paused for a moment, clearly enjoying the suspense, then said, "But listen to this: the letter isn't signed."

Millicent gripped the handles of her rocking chair. "My goodness. Who does he think it is from?" Oh, how could something so innocent go so wrong?

"Like I said, he doesn't know. We're going to do a little investigative work, though, try to figure it out."

Oh, Lord. She felt faint, she really did. Perhaps her corset was too tight? "Oh, my . . ."

Chrissie appeared then, a cup of tea in hand for George. "Figure what out?"

"Thanks." George took the tea from Chrissie, his fingers lingering on hers for a moment before returning to the conversation at hand. "Oh, I was just telling Millicent about Marshall's mysterious note."

"A note?"

George smiled with glee, obviously pleased by Marshall's unexpected turn of events. "A note from a strange woman, offering her company for a picnic." His eyes flickered, as if he was imagining the scene before him. "Sounds intriguing, don't it?"

Millicent couldn't help but take exception to George's exaggeration. She was just about to tell him so when Chrissie turned to her in surprise.

"Do you know anything about this?" she asked, surely waiting for Millicent to tell the full story.

Millicent knew this was the perfect opportunity to correct Marshall's wrong assumption. She could even laugh it off, and blame it on the wind, or some such foolishness.

But, she didn't. Instead she gave Chrissie a look that her friend knew well. A well-meaning look that spoke volumes and recalled past secrets. "No," Millicent said to Chrissie as firmly as she was able. "I know nothing of a note inviting *Marshall* to a picnic. If I was the type of woman to invite men to picnics, why, I am sure I would at least have the forethought to sign my name." She placed a palm against her breast for good measure. "I mean, can you even imagine such audacity?"

Chrissie sputtered. "But, Mill . . ."

Obviously Chrissie had forgotten the aforementioned meaning behind their secret look. "Hmm," she said instead.

George looked a little uncomfortable. "Course, *you* couldn't imagine it, Miss Millicent. I mean, I doubt *you've* ever had to stoop so low as to extend an invitation to any man, if you'll pardon me for saying so."

"But, George—" Chrissie tried to interject.

Millicent deftly cut her off, a pleased smile curving her lips. "Thank you for that, George. But just because I haven't had to resort to those measures doesn't mean I object to them. Um, perhaps it was just a mix-up? Perchance the note just, ah . . . blew his way?" At his doubtful expression, she added, "Maybe he received the note accidentally?"

"It was under a rock, right next to his door, Millicent," George corrected. "That note was meant for him."

"Well," Millicent said weakly, wondering how her innocent gesture ended up under his rock. "Isn't this interesting. But it's certainly nothing to get too excited about. I mean, my goodness . . . stranger things have happened here in Rocky River."

George shrugged, a sparkle belying his indifference. "Maybe, but Marshall's mighty interested. I saw him finger that note quite a bit. And he's mentioned at least a half-dozen women who could be the author."

"A half-dozen women?" A fresh, unwelcome wave of jealousy coursed through Millicent. "He's not actually going to go to the picnic, is he?"

"He's thinking about it, as a matter of fact," George said, grinning at Chrissie. "I kind of think he's liking the attention."

"The attention? Marshall doesn't need more attention,"

Millicent said firmly. "He's always had his full share of notice from the ladies in town!" Then, noticing Chrissie's arched eyebrow, she added, "or so I have heard."

Chrissie sat down on a rocker. "What do you mean by 'attention', George?"

George's eyes sparkled. "Well, it created quite a stir when he announced to the men at the Dark Horse that he meant to find this secret woman, come hell or high water before the appointed picnic."

"What?"

"It's true," George said, serious as can be. "He wants to have some idea of just who this mystery woman is before he decides to picnic with her."

"My goodness." Millicent was sure a headache was coming on.

George was positively glowing. "It was a sight to see. Next thing we knew, men were placing bets and making guesses about the identity of the secret author."

Chrissie smiled at the description. "You don't say?"

"Yep. Matter of fact, when Graham Moore started buying everyone a round of drinks, Marshall even went so far as to proclaim that the letter was the best piece of mail he had received in a whole month, business was so good."

"Is that right?"

"Of course, Edward VanHusen said that letter had nothing on the dime novels he had received all the way from San Francisco . . ." George's voice trailed off. "Pardon me, ladies," he said, cheeks coloring. "Never you mind that."

Chrissie looked determined to get the full story. "So, George, you're saying that Marshall's determined to find the author of this note before Sunday?"

"Yep. He's got a personal stake in it now. It's become a matter of honor. I mean, there's a betting pool going."

"Oh, my," Millicent said weakly.

Minutes later, after George left, Millicent became busy with the folds in her skirt to avoid the look in Chrissie's eyes. Unfortunately, she couldn't avoid her censured tone, too.

"Millicent, what is going on? Why didn't you tell George the truth, that it was your note, meant for me?"

What could she say? She truly didn't know why. "How're you going to cook that trout?"

"Millicent," Chrissie said firmly, "you can't get out of this."

She lifted her gaze skyward. "Oh, heavens, I don't know. Just all of a sudden, I didn't want Marshall knowing I wrote it. Don't worry, nothing will come of it."

Chrissie set her cup of tea on the floorboards, propped her elbows on her knees, and looked directly at her friend. "I'd say something already has," she said firmly. "What if he finds out that it was your handwriting, and comes over to ask you about it?"

"He won't."

"But if he does?"

Millicent felt her cheeks heat. "Well . . . I'd . . . just tell him the truth, right then and there."

"You don't think he'd find it strange that you didn't tell him so right away?"

"For heaven's sake, I don't know what you expect me to do. After all, all we really know is what George said was being talked about in the saloon. No respectable lady would even pretend she knew what that conversation was."

Chrissie looked at her with misgiving. "Millicent. This is Rocky River, not Saint Louis! Everyone knows every conversation that occurs in a public place, and most of the private ones, as well. It's part of our town's charm."

"I don't believe that includes saloons."

"Oh, honestly," Chrissie harrumphed.

Millicent knew she was grasping at straws, but at this point, she knew it was better than nothing. "I'm an upstanding citizen, Chrissie. I've got a reputation to uphold."

"Goodness, sometimes I just don't know where you pull that high horse of yours out from!" Chrissie exclaimed. "You and I both know there's not a soul in town who would fault you for listening to George's tale, or attempting to correct it."

Millicent tried to sit up straighter, no mean feat in a rocking chair. "Please don't tell George the truth, Chrissie," she pleaded. "I don't want anyone thinking I wrote Marshall a secret note . . . or Marshall to realize that he's confused about receiving attention. It will be better if we just let this thing run its course. After all, it will all end when no one shows up to picnic on Sunday, anyway."

Chrissie opened her mouth to retort, then closed it just as quickly. "Oh . . . very well."

Millicent smiled. "Thank you. Well, I'd better get going and leave you to your fish."

"Pa does love his fried trout."

"I'll leave you then. Goodbye, Chrissie, and thanks."

"You're welcome, though I have a feeling I might regret keeping my silence. See you tomorrow."

Chapter Three

Millicent straightened her skirt as she made her way down the sidewalk, past the twelve houses that stood between Chrissie's and her own . . . and almost walked right into Marshall himself.

He held out two hands to hold her steady when they almost collided. "Excuse me, Miss Millicent. I didn't see you," he said with a grin.

She had the grace to laugh; after all, it had been she who had not been paying attention. "Pardon me, I guess I was lost in thought."

He tipped his hat, then turned toward her just as she was about to walk away. "Miss Millicent, may I speak with you for a moment?"

Her palms began to itch and her heart beat fervently. She couldn't honestly say if it was from his words or his proximity. "Of course, Marshall."

He looked as if he was going to speak, then glanced around the street in mild annoyance. "May I walk you home? There's something on my mind that I'd like to share."

Perhaps Marshall also felt there was little hope of private conversation in public places. "Of course."

Nodding in response, he stepped next to her, grasping her elbow when they approached a muddy spot. "Careful," he murmured. His touch was sure, comforting. Millicent couldn't deny that she was pleased when he didn't remove his hand as they walked farther.

Heat radiated from his palm and filled her with warmth. A sudden vision of that same hand, caressing her—this time bare to his touch—crossed her mind, and she coughed in consternation. Why had no one else's touch ever caused such thoughts to appear?

To fill the void of silence, she spoke. "I must say that the day is quite mild for April."

"Yes ma'am, it is," he answered politely.

They walked a few more steps, Marshall shortening his long strides to match hers. "I believe Mr. Raymond said he didn't expect snow for at least another week."

"Ranchers will appreciate that, I expect."

"Yes, I believe so," she replied then mentally cringed. Goodness. What was she talking about? She'd had more scintillating conversation with sheep! However, she was well aware of the train of her thoughts. She was a bundle of nerves waiting for him to tell her what was on his mind. What did he want to speak with her about? A Saturday night date? Maybe he wanted to come courting?

Millicent glanced in his direction again. Did he know she wrote the note already? Was her handwriting that distinctive, like Chrissie said? Was he going to chide her for it, tell her that it was far too bold of a thing for a woman of esteemed reputation to do?

As they approached her house, Marshall guided her to the front porch swing, then stood in front of her like a sentry. She waited.

"Miss Millicent, it's like this: I received a note today."

She widened her eyes demurely. "Yes?"

"It was of a personal nature." He glanced at her, then focused on a spot above her head as he continued. "I'm hoping that since we've known each other for so long . . ."

"Yes?"

"That perhaps you'd give me some advice on a certain matter."

She pinched the skin between her thumb and forefinger, and tried to sound concerned, not worried. "Mm hmm?" she croaked.

He glanced at her in surprise, then back above her head again. "Millicent, it seems that I have a secret admirer. I'm not quite sure what to do about it."

Here was her opportunity to come clean and save herself from a world of hurt. "Is that right?" she asked innocently instead. She paused for a moment, then plunged ahead. "You know, come to think of it, I do believe George mentioned something about you receiving a note earlier this afternoon."

He looked relieved that she already knew. "Any idea who could have written it?"

Lord help her. "I couldn't guess, Marshall."

Those brown eyes of his sparkled at her words. "I guess you couldn't." He rocked on the balls of his feet and looked out above her head once more. "See, the thing of it is, I've been doing quite a bit of thinking about this note . . . and I think my receiving it might be considered a sign."

She swallowed hard. "A sign?"

He nodded. "Yep." He glanced at the vacant two feet of swing and sat down beside her. Immediately Millicent caught a whiff of bay rum and her insides did a somersault. Oh, no one smelled as good as Marshall Bond.

Thank goodness he didn't seem to be aware of her intense reaction. "See, business is going real good now . . . and I've been thinking for some time that it might be high time to take a wife."

Millicent adjusted her body next to his and tried not to become distracted by his proximity. But he smelled so good, it was hard to ignore, and heat seemed to radiate from him. What would he feel like up close, in his arms?

Then his words penetrated her mind. *Take a wife*? Oh my. He truly had come courting! For heaven's sakes, was he already proposing? "My goodness," she gasped.

He seemed unaware of her exclamation. "Ever since I made the decision to stay here and start up the Dark Horse and not go to California with my family, I've been biding my time until I could honestly say that I was making a decent living."

She recalled when his parents and two brothers left, four years ago. Marshall's decision to become his own man, build his own dreams, had been a hard one. He had worked hard in Rocky River and had developed a good reputation through honesty and hard work.

She knew his parents had been proud of him . . . and that they told him so in their frequent letters. Whenever Marshall had talked of goals, Millicent had always heard him speak of expanding his business, or improving the saloon.

But this . . . this talk of marriage was a new development. Maybe he'd always had a secret admiration for her also and she had never, ever known it?

Marshall kept talking, unaware of her jumbled thoughts. "I decided I ought to take this note appearing on my doorstep seriously and make some plans."

She was so full of emotion she could only nod.

He continued on. "If some lady is already interested in me . . . so interested that she's resorting to writing me secret notes . . . well, that's half the battle in the game of love, don't you think?"

Yes, her mind screamed. Instead she merely nodded and tried to look reasonable. Maybe it was fate that led her note to Marshall's doorstep! Maybe that wind was going to turn Marshall Bond in her direction and they would be together, always.

"I need to find out who this lady is . . . she may be my best chance for a family and future happiness."

Oh, what a pickle! What could she tell him? That she had secretly admired him for years? That she recalled the one time they had waltzed together, at Peggy Sue Johnston's wedding two years ago? That a thrill went through her whenever he took her arm or gazed at her with those lovely, lovely dark brown eyes? That her mouth practically watered every time he came near?

Taking a deep breath, she steadied herself to speak, already knowing that there was only one way that she could possibly respond. "Marshall, may I be frank? I believe that any number of ladies would be interested in assuming that, er, position in your life." There. She had practically thrown her interest in his face!

"Any number of ladies?" He grinned sardonically. "Well, thank you for that."

Anytime, Millicent thought grimly.

They swung for another moment; Millicent unsure of what to say next; Marshall looking like he had more to say but didn't know how to get started. Her heart went out to him. After all, she could only imagine the stress of proposing to a woman . . . wondering how she would respond to his question. Mentally she prepared herself to accept his proposal demurely and let him take her in his arms . . . finally press his lips to hers.

She would be responsive, but ladylike. Passionate but firm that they needed to wait until their wedding night before they allowed their baser instincts to get ahold of them. It would be difficult, she knew, but with prayer, they could manage to be patient. After all, they had already waited this long.

After several more swings, he finally spoke. "Millicent, honey . . ."

"Yes?"

"Would you mind . . . would you consider . . ."

Her pulse raced. She forced herself to look calm and composed. "Yes, Marshall?" she prodded dreamily.

"Looking at my list?"

Her head snapped to the right. "Your list?"

"Yes." He reached into his coat pocket and pulled out a grungy slip of paper. "After careful consideration, I came to the conclusion that no woman is going to come right out and say she wrote me the note, so I decided to be assertive, so to speak."

"Assertive?"

He unfolded the paper. "See, after I received the note, I

spoke to some people about it in the saloon, and then things got a little harried. Before I knew it, why, everyone had something to say about the author as well as taking a wife." He grimaced as if the memory was vaguely distasteful. "So, in between the betting pools, I wrote down twelve women who I thought not only could have written the note but also might make me a suitable wife."

"List? Twelve?" She was so snapping mad, she felt sure that if she pushed hard enough he would fall off her swing. Maybe even get hurt.

He continued as if she hadn't spoken. "I thought I'd take them out, to lunch and dinner, and so forth, and see if any of them suit." He paused for a moment. "What do you think?"

What did she think? Truly, what could she say? That she wrote the note, to someone else? That he was completely mistaken in thinking that he had a secret admirer? That he had just completely missed his chance to propose to her and look forward to a lifetime of future happiness? She bit her lip. None of those were good choices. She loved Marshall and didn't want to hurt his feelings for anything. Millicent sighed. She just couldn't do it. "I'd be happy to look at your list."

With a relieved grin, he smoothed out the paper and presented it to her with a flourish.

She grasped it with trepidation.

Then gasped when she read the list of names. Twelve women . . . each one with a chance of being Marshall's prospective bride.

Not a one of them her own. "Marshall, some of these women cannot even read, let alone write you an invitation," she said testily.

He actually looked offended. "Come now, Millicent. Just because all of the women don't prescribe to your high moral standards doesn't mean, that they wouldn't make suitable wives."

Immediately she took umbrage to his words. "I guess it depends what their qualifications needed to be."

Marshall reddened. "Millicent, there's not a thing wrong with any of these women."

"There's not much good," she bit out, then was immediately ashamed. That wasn't quite true. Some of the girls listed were actually very nice. And in addition, they were also her sisters in prospective matrimony. Well, so to speak. Honestly, what was wrong with her?

His eyes narrowed. "I'm sure they would be proud to go out to dinner with me."

"Since there's food involved, I believe you are exactly right."

"Millicent."

She gripped the paper tighter. All she could do was imagine Marshall taking these women out, enjoying private conversation with them. Taking their arms in the twilight . . . flashing those perfect, white teeth across a table. Jealousy coursed through her like a bad meal. She clamped it down firmly. Only then did she trust herself to speak her mind. "Why isn't my name on this list?"

He looked taken off guard. "Excuse me?"

"Well, if everyone on the list isn't also a suspected author of the note, why didn't you add my name to it?"

"Are you saying that you wrote the note?"

"I didn't say that," she said honestly.

His adam's apple was working overtime. "Millicent, these are prospective *brides*."

"You don't think I'm qualified for that position?"

"Come now, Miss Mill, surely you wouldn't be interested in . . ."

Her eyes met his directly. "I wouldn't be interested in marriage, a family . . ."

"In me."

If he only knew. "Well, now, I wouldn't rightly know, would I?" she asked, not quite able to keep the hurt out of her voice. "You've yet to take me out on a Saturday night."

Marshall snatched back his paper. "Even if I had it in mind to ask you, Millicent, you're always booked up weeks in advance!"

"So?"

"So? How's a man to act, being made to feel like he's only the next in line?"

"Next in line?"

He turned to her more squarely. "And it's public knowledge that you've yet to go out with any of them more than once."

"Now, that is not my fault . . . there were extenuating circumstances for some."

"I'll just bet," he said dryly.

"In any case . . ."

"Besides, I have a saloon to run," he said, cutting her off. "I can't be making plans so far in advance."

Millicent hopped up from the swing and faced him. "You don't have to make up excuses for your lack of attention, Marshall. It's not as if I've been losing sleep over your negligence. I'm sure one of those women on your list would suit *you* just fine."

His fingers gripped the edge of the swing, as if in a desperate quest for control. Millicent stood above him and tried not to look lovestruck and desperate at the same time. Eventually both of their breathing slowed and each searched the other's expression for signs of forgiveness. Marshall's gaze softened first.

"I can't believe we're having this conversation," he chuckled.

Although she felt herself capitulating, she wasn't quite ready to admit it. "Might I remind you that you are the one who suggested it?"

A wicked gleam entered his eyes. "I needed your advice."

"Well, you have received it."

"Honestly, Millicent," he said, shaking his head. "You can be ornerier than a goat! Just for that, I'm going to put you on my list."

A flutter went through her breast. "How kind of you," she said mockingly. "And when is my chosen meal to be?"

His eyes narrowed. "I'll let you know. I'm going to put you at the very end of my list—make you wait for a date for a change."

Oh, how the humiliation made her seethe! "How thoughtful. Would you like to be placed on mine? I think there's a Saturday open in June."

He stood up. "I think not."

Another unexplained burst of indignation ran through her. She jutted out her chin. "Well, then, I guess there's nothing left for us to say. Good bye."

He slammed his hat on his head. "Good bye," he returned, then strode to her front walkway before turning back to her. "And may I add that you look very fetching today in pink."

A hand rested on her hip. "Thank you," she said, meeting

his gaze once again, her heart hammering in her ears. "I just finished making it yesterday."

They stood facing each other for a moment, then began to chuckle in unison. "I'll be seeing you, Miss Millicent," he called out.

"I certainly hope so," she whispered back.

Chapter Four

Marshall sauntered away from Millicent's house with no more information than he had had when he was walking the other way. Of all the conversations he'd had with her, why this one was surely the strangest. Imagine telling Millicent that she was going to be added to his list. As if they would ever suit.

His mouth twisted wryly as he thought of their previous interactions. Her prissy attitude always brought out a strange, foreign nature inside of him. He couldn't number the times when he wasn't both put off and attracted to her quick wit and holier-than-thou demeanor. There was something about the way those blue eyes sparkled when she had her backbone up. He had to remind himself that she wasn't the girl for him. Matter of fact, he was sure he had no use for someone who put on so many airs when she was just a common seamstress.

In spite of himself, he winced at his words.

Oh yes—she was more than that. There was not a common thing about her. She was the reason men went to the west for more money and a brighter future. She was the reason men paid to get a decent bath on a Saturday night. Millicent Drovers was everything a man envisioned when he envisioned courting. Perfect manners. Delicate sensibilities. Full lips. Thick, long hair that was always pinned up. It made a man ache to see it down, flowing across her shoulders. Millicent made a man want to slow his pace and curb his language and go to church. Well, most men, himself not included, Marshall was honest enough to admit.

Miss Millicent's starched dresses and composed demeanor set him a little on edge. He wanted to mess her up a little bit and see what she'd do. Take her out riding and watch her get hot and bothered. Talk to her about things other than the weather, and watch her sensibilities get frazzled. Run his fingers through that hair, kiss her senseless, feel her in his arms, see if her bosom was really as full as it seemed to be.

Just the thought of it got him riled up.

Which, after all, was exactly the reason he had avoided her little Saturday night engagements. He didn't trust himself to be the gentleman around her. He'd been her friend for years, and had tried to look out for her since her pa had died. He felt funny thinking of her in a way that wasn't strictly brotherly. Not when he had other things in mind that were far from that.

As he approached the town square, he tipped his hat to a group of ladies in front of the mercantile, and nodded in the direction of Sheriff Merry. Then he was halted by Edmund Baxter, owner of one of Rocky River's most profitable mines.

Edmund had a taste for whiskey, gossip, and loose

women, and not necessarily in that order. And those were his good points. It was common knowledge that a strange fluke in providence had somehow elevated Edmund Baxter from the town's most notorious lowlife to a wealthy mine owner with the stroke of an ax.

It was a true testament to his personality and grooming habits that most people still avoided him at all costs.

"Baxter," Marshall nodded.

Edmund Baxter fixed his beady eyes on Marshall. "I hear you got some interesting mail today."

"You could say that."

"Hear you got a bet going, too."

"Now, that bet is not my doing."

Edmund inserted two dirty nails into the waistband of his trousers, hooking the pants up. "But you're encouraging it."

Marshall nodded. "Men like a good wager. I'm thinking it will be good for business."

"Any idea who the author is?"

"Not a one."

A flicker of interest entered Edmund's eyes, though they were kind of hard to see, on account of a stringy lock of blond hair that swung in front of them, like a pendulum. "I saw you walking Miss Drovers home just now," Edmond said. "Never saw you do that before."

What was he getting at? "And?"

"Maybe Miss Drovers wrote you that note."

Marshall's stomach clenched. For some reason, he didn't think much of Edmund speaking of Millicent. "I think not. Actually, I was hoping for some advice from her."

Edmund scowled. "Bet you didn't get much. I've been trying to get a date with her for months. She's always booked up." He spit on the ground for emphasis. "Who does she think she is, anyway? Awful high and mighty for a girl that takes in clothes."

Marshall's eyes narrowed. "I'd watch your mouth if I were you. Miss Drovers is a real fine lady."

"She may be a lady in her mind, but she's still a woman, if you know what I'm saying," Edmund sneered. "It'd do her good to get a little reminder of just who she is from someone."

Marshall grabbed Edmund by the collar. The man's eyes widened from the snug grasp. "I wouldn't even think of walking on the same side of the street as her, Baxter. You got no business taking notice of a woman like that."

"Seems to me that there's no law preventing a man to speculate about her uh, charms," Edmund replied, his smile showing a remarkable lack of incisors.

Their argument drew the notice of several others standing nearby. A few spectators stepped closer, ready to give Marshall a hand.

But Marshall was in no hurry to ask for help. "I better not hear you speak of her in that way again."

"Or you'll do what?" Edmund blustered.

"Or I'll kick your backside hard enough that you'll wish you had a bigger one," Marshall hissed.

As expected, Edmund's eyes widened and took a step back. "Look, just because I've seen some hard times doesn't mean I ain't good enough for her."

"You cussed fool . . ."

Grumbling drifted out from the crowd.

George stepped closer. "You need a hand here, Marshall?"

His friend's appearance brought him back to reality.

Stunned, Marshall stared at the crowd in shock. Expectant faces peered back at him, all ready to see blood shed. He forced himself to take a deep breath.

What was he doing, getting ready to fight over Millicent Drover's good name? He wasn't the type of man to brawl in the street! Disgusted with himself, Marshall shook his head. "Nah, I was just heading to the saloon."

George glanced at Edmund, then back at Marshall's stiff posture. "I was just thinking about getting a drink myself. Mind if I join you?"

Marshall glared at Edmund one last time, then turned away. "Let's go. There's nothing here worth wasting our time on."

"You just wait, Marshall," Edmund called out with considerable more gumption. "Just you wait to see what happens now."

Marshall ignored him, instead using all of his control to make his way to the saloon. "Darn coot," he muttered.

As the entered the saloon, Marshall immediately felt the muscles in his back relax. The dim light and familiar smells wafted to him. A few cowboys were playing poker at a back table. Sadie, his best bargirl, nodded a greeting. And Frank, his bartender for the last three years, raised a hand at their appearance.

In two hours, the place would begin to heat up and get busy. But for now, it was Marshall's favorite time. The few people lent the building life, but it was low-key for the moment . . . lazy. He and George sat down at a table near the bar, and when Sadie appeared, he only asked for a beer.

"What was that all about?" George asked when they were alone. "Haven't seen you so riled up since the time Ancil

Weever drank a bottle of whiskey and tried to take off without payin'.' "

Marshall reached into his coat pocket for a cheroot, and lit it with little aplomb. "Nothing. He was talking trash about someone. I got tired of hearing about it."

George smiled at Sadie when she arrived with their beers and took a moment to ask her about her two-year-old son. "That's Edmund, all right," he replied after licking the foam from the top of the glass. "Don't worry about it. He's always running his mouth off."

"It's about to get him in trouble."

George laughed. "Heck, it already has. Remember last month? Sadie had Sheriff Merry toss him in the jail for a few hours."

Marshall nodded, but was uncomfortably aware of where his thoughts were headed. "What was he doing again?"

"Grabbing her backside. Speakin' lewdly. Wouldn't leave her alone." George chuckled at the memory. "After a good thirty minutes, Sadie'd had enough! She marched right over to Merry and told him in no uncertain terms what he needed to do with Baxter."

"Sadie has no problem taking care of herself. You'd think Baxter would have realized that by now. My girls don't give out favors."

"He knows, now!" George cackled, then sobered, his gaze speculative. "So . . . is that who Edmund was talkin' about, Sadie?"

Marshall puffed on the cigar again. "Nope. It was someone else. Millicent."

George sat up. "What? Everyone knows Miss Millicent wouldn't have anything to do with the likes of him."

"Everyone knows it but Baxter. It seems he's a little peeved about waiting his turn for her."

"Waiting for his turn?"

Marshall shrugged. "Waiting for *a* turn, I guess more like it. She hasn't registered him on her dating calendar yet."

"But why'd he talk to you about it?"

Marshall shrugged. "He saw me walking with her, thought I was courting her."

"Well, I'll be." George sipped on his beer as he regarded his friend, a slow smile cracking his otherwise somber expression. "Are you?"

"Of course not. I was only walking with her to get her opinion on this letter, that's all."

"What'd she say?"

"She had no inkling. But she thought my dinner dates were a fine idea."

"Speaking of which, you going out with Millicent anytime soon?"

Marshall scowled. "As a matter of fact, we spoke about that."

"And . . ."

"She seemed a little put off that she wasn't on my dating list."

"Is that right?"

"So I told her she could be added at the end."

George laughed. "I bet that got her gander up."

"You could say that," Marshall smiled, recalling the way those blue eyes of hers had been spitting mad. " 'Course, now I'm wondering if perhaps I ought to take her out sooner, let Baxter know he has no business even thinking about her."

George sobered. "You think he'd try?"

"He's getting impatient."

"She's a good woman. She don't deserve his unwanted attentions."

"I know that."

"Heck, I don't believe she'd even know what to do if Edmund tried anything disrespectful."

The sudden vision of Edmund Baxter trying to touch Millicent brought a hard chill through him. What if Baxter did try to attack her? Would she be able to defend herself? And if she couldn't? What could she do? She'd not only be devastated, but ruined to boot! Someone needed to look out for her. "He better not try anything."

George looked at him steadily for a moment before speaking. "So, what are you going to do?"

"I'm just going to take her out myself."

"When? Her Saturday nights are already taken—and you know you can't be leaving here on a Friday."

"I'll figure out something. Maybe take her on a picnic."

George's eyes widened. "When? You've already got to go picnic with your mystery woman!"

Marshall threw his head back in frustration. "Shoot. I'll find sometime to take her out. I plumb forgot about Sunday."

"You forgot?" George wheezed. "That's the whole reason you saw Miss Millicent in the first place!"

"I know it."

"You need to get your mind back on track."

Marshall's mouth twisted. "There's just too many little dramas playing out in my life right now."

"Well, that is a fact . . ." A slow grin spread across George's face. "And you know what? You just happen to be playin' a part in all of them." He tucked a finger in his vest and looked in appreciation as Ernestine, Marshall's piano player, entered the area and began to play with a flourish. "Thing is, you've got a picnic on Sunday to go to, come hell or high water." George pulled out a wad of money and stared at it meaningfully. "Lotta people countin' on that picnic."

"Lot of people are counting their wallets, you mean."

George merely shrugged. "All I'm sayin' is that Millicent and her troubles are just going to have to be put on hold until you get your mystery woman figured out."

Marshall took a slow drag from the cheroot as he examined his friend speculatively. "How much did you end up betting?"

"Enough."

Marshall rolled his eyes, then shifted uneasily as he recalled something shifty in Baxter's demeanor. That man had been up to something, and it wasn't good. He couldn't be trusted around Millicent. She was going to need some help fending him off. And he, for some unknown reason, had volunteered to do the helping. 'Course, they were friends—had been for some time, as a matter of fact. How could he just sit back and let some lowlife paw her?

Irritated with the chain of events, he slammed down his cigar. "Shoot . . ." he moaned. "How come providence has chosen this point and time to come into my life?"

"A man just can't help himself against divine intervention," George answered prophetically, then leaned back against his chair and looked at his friend in bemusement. "All things considered, I'd say your life has just got pretty interestin'."

As for that, Marshall could only agree.

Chapter Five

Evening engagements were the farthest thing from Millicent's mind the next morning when she took out her sewing basket and Mrs. Alexander's dress. In a rare bout of goodwill, Mr. Alexander had allowed his wife to have two dresses made for the spring season, and the lady had given Millicent the job, provided she could finish one of the gowns in just a week.

Mrs. Alexander was a handsome woman with an easy, chatty personality and aspirations toward new fashions. Four days ago she had arrived at Millicent's doorstep with a bolt of fabric and a *Godey's Lady's Book*, full of local gossip and plans for a new gown. The designs were so pleasing, Millicent was delighted to sew the dresses.

They were to be in the latest styles, with high bustles and a minimum of lace. The first was to be a lovely sea green day dress. The second was a gown of light blue in a heavy damask, the epitome of simplicity. Rows of pleats sewn on the bodice and skirt gave the gown a modern flair.

36

Unfortunately, she had been so wrapped up in the excitement of the note and meeting with Marshall that Millicent had not spared a thought for the dress the day before. Now she had one day to piece it together before Mrs. Alexander's fitting at ten o'clock Friday morning.

Millicent mentally berated herself for her foolishness as she continued to pin together the pieces and painstakingly sewed the seams.

'Course, some would say this foolishness was all her fault. If she hadn't been so silly, she could have simply told George the truth, spared Marshall the trouble of his dating campaign, and gone about her business without a second thought. But things hadn't happened that way.

Smoothing out the fabric on the table, Millicent tried to think of the point in time when everything had gotten so twisted in her life. She chewed on her lip. When had she suddenly thought of Marshall in a way that wasn't purely platonic?

Had it been when she had first waltzed with Marshall two years ago, and he had held her so firmly in his arms?

Or when Anderson Herglesburger had asked her out and she had first hoped for a reason to say no? Or when he tipped his hat to her and she hoped to one day touch his dark hair?

Or when her pa had died and he had held her close and told her that he'd keep her safe?

When had things with Marshall gotten so confusing?

She really couldn't say. All she could say was that she had a powerful attraction for Marshall Bond that was too strong to ignore, and too close to her heart to go away.

Taking care to keep her stitches even, she recalled the

last time she had danced with him, three months ago, at the harvest dance.

He'd had on a crisp white shirt and black vest. She'd worn her yellow gown with the grand leg-o-mutton sleeves. He'd gone up to her chair, where she had been sitting with Chrissie. He'd taken off his hat and politely asked her to dance.

Then his hand had stretched out to hers, and she had taken it readily, his palm feeling so firm and cool in her own.

Other people had called out greetings, but he had ignored them, choosing to only focus on her. And his lips had twitched when he had placed his hand around her waist and felt her shiver at his touch.

Millicent's fingers stilled as she captured the moment once again in her mind. When the fiddle had started, he had stepped forward with ease, and glided her through the maze of dancers. He had smelled like bay rum and tobacco, and his oh-so-lovely eyes had been serious when they had looked into her own. She had felt the muscles in his arm tighten when they had spun around again and again, just like little girls twirling in a wide field.

And once, when another couple had passed too closely, Marshall had pulled her next to him, and she'd had the novel sensation of brushing her whole body next to his. He'd felt hot, and solid, and tantalizing. She'd had the urge to press herself against him, feel her chest against his own . . . just to see what it would feel like . . . but then he stepped back abruptly, a faint flush coloring his cheeks.

"Beg pardon, ma'am," was all that he said.

And she'd just stared open-mouthed in wonder at his words, like a deceased fish.

All too soon, the dance finished and Marshall had returned her to the spot next to Chrissie. Then he'd left, presumably to check on things at the Dark Horse, though she couldn't say why . . . most of Rocky River's population was dancing with them in the field.

Sighing, Millicent bent toward her work again, smoothing the fabric with her fingers for an instant. Oh, she had felt grand in Marshall's arms. Instinctively, she knew that was where she wanted to be again. That was where she needed to be.

She just didn't know how to get there.

After all, what was a single girl to do, with only a stellar reputation and pair of good eyes to attract his notice? Although she had always been proud of her pa, she was well aware that a miner's daughter with little money to speak of and no family to call her own put her in a precarious spot in society. Her common sense told her that she should have eagerly accepted the first man's attentions to her and married quickly. She needed to ensure a future for herself.

But she hadn't. Something was missing when she went out with all those men on her Saturday night dates. Something was missing when they spoke with her about their jobs, and their families, and their dreams.

Marshall.

Now she had no idea how to encourage his interest, to switch his attentions from brotherly to lover-like. But there had to be a way.

Because one thing was for sure: If Marshall had made up his mind to begin courting multiple women . . . she needed to make sure that she was one of the numbers!

Perhaps she needed to rearrange her schedule and fit him in on a Saturday night real soon. She just didn't trust all those women after him. After all, *she* was the reason he was going courting in the first place!

Honestly, if someone needed to take fate in their hands . . . well, it might as well be her.

Chapter Six

Rocky River had one locale that separated it from the rest of the mining towns, in terms of gentility and refinement. The opera house.

Well, they didn't actually sing opera there—more like regular songs—most of which were familiar to everyone there, miners, ranchers, and travelers alike.

And, it wasn't a house, per se, more like a square building with an elaborate facade. Some passersby had made the mistake of commenting that it was a poor substitute for the music halls in St. Louis or even Denver, for that matter. Local folk didn't care for that description, however. The Opera House was their crowning achievement in a quest for civility, and no one was to find fault with it.

Certainly not Millicent, although she feared she could have done without seeing each musical performed four and five times. Most every Saturday night date took place there, each gentleman not wanting to look cheap in the competition's eyes. She feared the actresses on stage even knew her face. Worse, she'd even heard rumors that the actors considered her presence a sign of good luck. Not that Millicent herself held much stock in those words.

But this Saturday evening, sitting on the right of Beauregard Hamlish, was looking to be long. Millicent wondered why she had even accepted his offer in the first place.

Demurely, she inspected him again. He was tall, but not well-muscled, having spent most of his days in a bank building in Cincinnati before venturing out west. He still had that citified air about him though, and his manners were as perfect as a lady could wish for. He had wavy brown hair, with hints of red in it, and a large mustache, which twitched often when he spoke. Which was a lot.

Millicent stifled a sigh. Mr. Hamlish seemed to feel he was the authority on most things—banking, farming, mining, and frontier life included. However, from what she could discern, he had an extremely limited knowledge of most things related to Colorado. Currently, he was discussing the pros and cons of the newfangled machinery the miners were using. She nodded politely as he expounded his point home. For the third time.

Then her breath caught as she spied Marshall seated at a far table, in a dim corner, with Hannah Parson. Marshall looked as if he had anything but mining on his mind. He wore a lover-like expression and a wry grin. Hannah was speaking, and Marshall looked as if he could listen to her prattle all night long. Then his eyes raised, and twinkled as he caught Millicent staring at him. Slowly his head moved a fraction and one dark eyebrow raised a quarter of an inch, then his lips curved into a devilish grin.

Millicent harrumphed. She knew exactly what that look had meant. He had seen her date and found fault with him.

Well, honestly, so had she . . . but there wasn't any reason that Marshall should rub it in, and from a distance, no less!

Mr. Hamlish had moved from mining to vivid descriptions of his journey west, seeming to think his story was unique. Millicent curled her toes in her kid shoe in frustration when she tried to speak but was rudely cut off.

In the distance, Hannah Parson giggled.

Millicent straightened her posture and directed a withering look toward Marshall, letting him know in no uncertain terms what she thought of his actions.

Marshall just grinned wider, showing an excellent set of straight, white teeth.

Ohh! But then the curtain raised, Hannah started to turn her head to see what had caught Marshall's interest, and Beauregard had finally noticed that she could care less about mining advancements or the hazards of Conestoga wagons.

She placed her best social smile on her face, pretended there was nowhere else she would rather be than watching *On the Way to Heaven* for the third time and demurely clasped her hands in her lap.

"Miss Millicent," Beau whispered just when the actors started singing the title's song, his mustache grazing her cheek as he leaned too near.

She jumped at his proximity. "Yes?"

"Are you enjoying yourself?"

"Of course I am," Millicent replied politely, all the while edging farther away. "You're so kind to take me here."

He leaned closer and puffed up visibly. "I'm just delighted. I've been looking forward to this for several weeks, as you well know."

How could she reply to that? "I, also."

"I hope I won't be forced to wait so long for your company the next time we step out, Miss Mill."

Next time? Millicent pretended not to hear. Instead she turned her chair and took an avid interest in the movements on the stage.

The actors were singing in a pyramid formation, the woman at the top teetering precariously. And, if Millicent recalled correctly, any minute now a cloud was going to pop out of the ceiling and the players were going to raise their heads in surprise. Millicent tapped her foot to the beat of the heavy playing on the piano.

After safely ascertaining that Beau had taken her heavy-handed hint about not wanting to converse, she carefully turned her head to check on Marshall. He had Hannah's hand clasped in his, and once more, Hannah looked enthralled! Marshall looked as if there was nowhere else that he'd rather be than snuggled next to her!

Feeling very alone, that same, unwelcome pang of jealousy came back, tenfold, quickly replaced by a sense of longing. What would it be like to one day be sitting at this theater and have her hand clasped in Marshall's? To feel his body next to hers, for almost two hours? To look forward to a good-night kiss from him? Or maybe more, she thought wickedly.

She sighed, and a shiver passed through her as she imagined being in his arms, feeling the rough planes of his cheeks against her own, imagining the brush of his lips . . .

Beau noticed. "Millicent," he said, practically loud enough for the actors to hear. "You cold?"

Abruptly she was brought back to the present. "No, Beau, I'm just fine."

He made a motion to take her hand. She clasped them

more firmly together and stoutly directed her attention to the stage again, just to let Beau know in no uncertain terms that she was not that kind of girl.

She held her hands firmly together also when he attempted to take one on their walk home. Beau was reduced to clasping her elbow, even when they made their slow walk home in the chilly mid-April night.

And when she and Beau said their goodnights, she merely nodded her head when he asked if he might call on her some time. After all, he could do that, couldn't he? It didn't mean she would be available. And then she climbed into her feather bed, feeling petty and annoyed with herself. She hoped the next day would be much better.

Millicent drifted off to sleep, visions of neat, organized days in her head, imagining sharing the porch swing with Marshall, thinking about dancing with Marshall one day soon.

But then her eyes opened once again.

Tomorrow was the picnic. What was she going to do?

Chapter Seven

Marshall knew one thing for sure, never again was he
going to air his private thoughts to a room full of men
drinking beer. How he had come from sharing a private
note with George to wandering the park, dodging women
in gingham and holding picnic baskets was surely one of
the Lord's wonders of the world. At least a dozen women
had come to the park and had spread their wares on brightly
colored quilts around them. Marshall had the impression of
stepping upon a human chessboard, just waiting to be taken
off by a marauding queen.

He smiled faintly at Alyson Thomas and hurriedly
walked on, aching for a place to rest but not daring to sit
down on any one lady's picnic area. George had appeared
at his doorstep just minutes before he was set to leave,
bearing the news that there was an abundance of women
at the park with a gleam in his eye. In one fell swoop,
Marshall had become Rocky River's most eligible bachelor.
It was as if receiving that note had placed him among the

pillars of society, a place where girls dreamed of aspiring. It was, unfortunately, a place he had no hope of climbing down from.

Now, as he patrolled the grassy expanse, Marshall felt as if he was on a wanted poster, he had so many pairs of eyes pinned on him now.

Frantically he looked to George for some much-needed moral support. Sure enough, there he was, leaning against a hickory tree, arms folded, wearing a smug expression. Marshall gritted his teeth and walked toward him.

"Come help me out," he hissed under his breath.

"With what? You're the man on parade."

"It wasn't supposed to be like this. I was just going to have a nice meal with an interested woman."

"Well, now you get to do it several times," George said practically. "Hope you're hungry."

Marshall peeked over his shoulder. Anna Jane Jacobs looked back at him, a plate of cold chicken placed tantalizingly on her blanket. "What should I do?"

"Well, if I was you, which I ain't, thank God," George said, slow as molasses, "I would just sit down with Anna Jane here and eat some chicken."

"But what about everyone else?"

"They'll come."

"What do you mean?"

George sighed as if he was planning strategies for the Union battle lines. "Look, you've got something these here women want—marriage in mind."

"But . . ."

George held up a patient hand. "Listen. Don't fret," he ordered. "It's a fact that neither Hannah nor Alyssa nor

Bethany are going to let Anna Jane have all of your attention."

"You think they'll come on over?"

"Surely they will."

"What will I do then?"

George sighed, as if he was tired of doing all the work. "Honestly, Marshall, what's wrong with you? Show some gumption! You're going to be pleasant to everyone and take mental notes for your list. See if any of these ladies strike your fancy."

Marshall knew something was wrong with the plan, but for the life of him, he just couldn't think of what it was. To his way of thinking, sitting in one spot was much better than being passed from lady to lady like a hot potato. "You wanna stay?"

George scanned the crowd, his eyes lighting up when he spied Georgia Clemens' arrival. "Certainly. If Georgia's here, then a dried apple pie is here, too."

"Chrissie won't mind?"

"Gosh, no. Chrissie knows my heart and my stomach have different priorities." He tilted his head toward Georgia one more time. "Come on, Marshall. If nothing else, you're about to eat some of the best cooking you'll have in a whole month of Sundays."

Marshall let out a heavy sigh. "That's reason enough. Well, let's get on with it, then." Putting on his most debonair facade, Marshall approached Anna Jane and asked if he might join her for a spell. In no time, he was sitting next to her, eating a chicken leg, and hearing about the merits of her father's business, the largest funeral home in the valley.

George kept the conversation hopping, away from being

too personal, and introduced the other women as they strolled up and began passing around biscuits, potato salad, and glasses of tea.

This was the scene Millicent observed when she appeared at three-thirty that afternoon. Her mouth opened, then shut again as she stared at the group of enterprising ladies. Why, there were women there that she knew for a fact couldn't write, let alone have the where-with-all to write an elegant invitation! Honestly, how could so many women have taken advantage of her private correspondence? It just didn't make sense.

Resolutely, she stepped forward, ready to give the crowd of women and Marshall himself a piece of her mind, when a knowing grin from Hannah Parson interrupted her plans.

Millicent turned to her, belatedly realizing that she had positioned herself a mere three feet from Hannah's outstretched blanket.

"You couldn't stay away either, Millicent?" Hannah said snidely. "One would think that at least you would have the decency to stay away from Marshall, or does he even interest you now?"

Millicent knew exactly where Hannah's barbed comment came from. Almost four months ago Scott Barkley, Hannah's steady beau, had declared himself in love with Millicent. Although Millicent had done nothing to encourage his departure, Hannah took his leaving hard. She blamed his abdication on Millicent, although Millicent knew for a fact that the real culprit had been an afternoon with Hannah's annoying mother. It seemed Scott couldn't fathom a lifetime with that particular lady as his mother-in-law and had looked at Millicent in a more favorite light, since both of her parents were deceased.

For an instant, Millicent regretted her strong defense of Hannah's tender feelings so long ago. After all, she had told Scott in no uncertain terms that she couldn't be happy with someone who would tread so heavily on another's affections.

Now, however, as Millicent was treated to Hannah's rapier-like words, it looked as if there was more to Scott's departure than a mere mother-in-law.

"Hannah, I'm sure I don't know what you are talking about," Millicent said as snippily as she was able to and still keep an eye on Marshall. At the moment it looked as if Alyson Thomas was plying him with a piece of fresh baked bread.

Hannah continued, undeterred. "I'm speaking of your quest to steal the hearts of Rocky River's menfolk and leave nothing but shattered remains in your wake."

Hannah had always had a flair for the dramatic. Millicent settled her hands on her hips. "I have done no such thing. As a matter of fact, I only came here today to see who would have been brazen enough to actually stoop so low to send men familiar invitations." Inwardly she cringed. Oh, her web of deceit was getting more and more tangled!

Hannah did not seem bothered by Millicent's stance. "I certainly did not send Marshall an invitation to picnic."

Millicent carefully raised one eyebrow. "But . . ."

"But I'm here because this was an opportunity too good to miss!" She sniffed. "You know just how eligible Marshall is, even if he is just a saloon keeper."

For some reason, Millicent felt honor bound to defend Marshall's honor. "Marshall Bond is not *just* a saloon keeper. He is a wonderful gentleman, and, I might add . . . the Dark Horse is the premier gentlemen's establishment in Rocky River."

"It's still just a saloon." Hannah eyed the person they were speaking of. "I wonder if Marshall will change professions once he settles down?"

"I don't see why he would," Millicent answered, surprised. "It's Marshall's livelihood, and it's been around for quite a while. Men like going there, and being a saloon owner makes him happy. Why, the Dark Horse is a destination for some folks in the valley!"

"Perhaps." Hannah sniffed. "However, being a saloon owner is certainly not a suitable occupation for a married man, now is it?"

Hannah's tone didn't set well at all. "I suppose that would depend on who he was married to."

"Good afternoon, ladies," Marshall interrupted.

"Marshall!" Millicent gasped. "I didn't see you approach us."

He looked from Hannah to Millicent slowly. "I can see that."

Hannah primped and held up her basket demurely. "I made a fresh batch of fried chicken and my famous buttermilk cake."

"How original," Millicent snapped.

"Oh, I'm sorry. Did you not bring anything to share, Millicent?" Hannah asked, her voice filled with false concern.

"No. I was just, ah, passing through."

Hannah managed to latch herself onto Marshall's arm like an overeager tick. "Oh, that's right," she said innocently. "You don't cook, do you?"

"I cook . . ."

Hannah batted her lashes at Marshall as she finished Millicent's sentence for her. "Just not very well."

Marshall looked uncomfortable with the women's exchange. "I'll be seeing you, Miss Mill," he murmured, then folded his elbow for Hannah to take more securely.

Unthinking, Millicent raised her hand, "All right . . . I'll be seeing you." But her voice faded as she realized that the other two had already left, without so much as a backwards glance.

Her face heated as she felt the gaze of a dozen women on her, each having witnessed her complete and total setdown by Marshall and Hannah.

Resolutely, she turned on her heel and sauntered away with as much grace as she could possibly muster. Oh, she wondered yet again, how had things gotten so completely, utterly mixed up?

Chapter Eight

Millicent went home and immersed herself in her work. Although she had finished the day dress on time, the other gown was sadly behind schedule. Mrs. Anderson was due in the morning for a fitting and Millicent still had to pin the bodice and the skirt together, as well as baste the hem. She had no business lollygagging at a picnic, she told herself sternly. If she didn't get her work done now, she'd be up all night working on the gown.

Mrs. Anderson had been so pleased with her work in the past . . . and the progress of the two dresses, and how the elegant designs flattered her figure, that she went ahead and ordered two more. One was going to be in a beautiful chartreuse sateen that would have to be ordered from Denver or Colorado Springs. The other was to be a fancy ball gown for a dance in the fall.

The two of them had giggled over the plans for her ball gown, declaring that it would have so much crinoline that it'd have trouble fitting into her Saratoga trunk! Mrs. Anderson had been sure that once her husband had seen the beautiful fabric, he wouldn't hardly even flinch when he got the bill.

'Course, now that Millicent was alone, her workload just rested on her shoulders like an overweight Persian cat. There was too much work to be done and fluff kept getting in the way.

She worked steadily through the late afternoon, only stopping when Chrissie came over to drop off some cookies.

"George just stopped by," Chrissie said testily, stopping in the kitchen to put the kettle on for tea.

Millicent glanced up, eyed Chrissie's expression, and went right back to stitching. "Is that right?"

"Seems he's sporting a mighty bad stomachache from eating way too much mediocre food at that dratted picnic, if I do say so myself."

"I will admit that there was a broad expanse of dishes at that picnic," Millicent said.

Chrissie readied herself a cup of tea. "I sincerely hope Marshall ate something," she said airily, "because I do believe that George tasted a good portion from every basket there."

Millicent hid a smile. "You sound a little peeved. Did George's attendance at the picnic bother you? George being in all those girls' company?"

"Goodness, no. Everyone in town knows that George only has eyes for me," Chrissie said with no small hint of pride. "I've just been a little jealous of his interest in the other girls' food."

Millicent laughed. "Oh, Chrissie."

Chrissie's expression softened. "I know . . . I'm being

silly." She sighed. "I think George needed to be at that picnic, anyway. There were way too many women and only one Marshall, and a skittish Marshall at that, if George's report can be trusted." She shook her head in wonder. "George said that lots of girls confided to him that they were pretty nervous about the whole picnic, especially since there were so many of them and only one, um . . . honored guest. Speaking to George gave them something to do while Marshall made his rounds from quilt to quilt."

Millicent accidentally pricked her finger. "The girls confided in their feelings about Marshall?"

"Oh, don't worry, Milly," Chrissie said as she made herself at home on the flowered settee. "George didn't hear anything alarming, just who's ready for marriage, and so forth."

"Did anyone claim to be the author of the note?"

"Not that George could tell. Who knows what all the men in the betting pools are going to do now! Some of those men were really counting on making some easy money."

"Hmmph."

Chrissie just smiled. "Don't worry, Millicent. I bet things will settle down shortly."

"I'm not so sure, now that I saw Marshall with that Hannah Parsons on Saturday night. They looked pleased as punch with each other. Things might just go from bad to worse before we even know it."

"If things get more tangled, at least you'll know why."

Millicent shrugged her shoulders at that piece of news. Chrissie couldn't be more right about that. "I will, at that," she said quietly. Then, she couldn't help but tease Chrissie a little bit. "Some of the pies did look awfully appetizing.

Did George confide in you about any other girl's secret recipes?"

Chrissie pursed her lips. "He didn't dare, especially after he mentioned that Georgia had made her dried apple pie."

"I do believe that pie won a blue ribbon at the last Founder's Day fair."

"I'll have you know that I know for a fact that that ribbon was given out in pity," Chrissie pointed out in indignation. "I know, because I had already won the ribbons for best pickles and best cake and overheard Mr. Ancil Weever say that the awards needed to be spread out a little."

Millicent knew better than to refute that, so she simply nodded in agreement. "Well, I'm glad that everything is going fine between you and George."

"What about yourself? You worried about Marshall?"

"Some, though I don't know why. Like I said, I did happen to spy him with Hannah Parson at the opera the other night."

"The night you went with Beauregard?"

They shared a smile. "Yes, indeed. I, ah, happened to see Hannah at the picnic today, as well. The two of them make a handsome couple. Maybe even a good match."

"You and Marshall would make a nice match, as well."

"Oh, Chrissie, I don't see how that could be. I've only entertained a few girlish dreams about him . . . there's nothing to tie us together. Not even as much as he and Hannah have together."

Chrissie looked skeptical. "But at the dance last fall . . . it sure seemed as if there was something there, between you two."

Memories of the dance came flooding back. Her body shivered at the memory. "I felt it, too. Oh, well, we'll see what happens. I do think that he's going to take me out to the opera soon, though."

"Really?"

"When we were sparring, and let our emotions get the best of ourselves, he said he was going to add me to his list of potential brides."

"Millicent!"

"It was all in good fun," Millicent promised. "At least I think it was. In any case, we're due to go out sooner or later. Perhaps I'll know then how things stand between us."

"You due to see him any time soon?"

"No, but I wouldn't be too surprised if I saw him in the next couple of days, if only for him to give me an update on his picnic situation."

Chrissie shook her head. "I sure hope you know what you're doing, Millicent, because you sound more mixed up than a bear awake in January."

Honestly, sometimes she felt that way, too! Oh, what was she going to do about her mixed-up feelings and Marshall's mixed-up letter?

Chrissie stayed for a good two hours, and before they knew it, the bodice had been neatly sewed to the skirt of Mrs. Anderson's shirtwaist.

Feeling accomplished and much better after spending time with her best friend, Millicent ate some dinner, and was just getting ready to sit by the fire and read when Marshall knocked on the door.

And then, before she knew it, they were sitting on her front porch and watching the sky, just like they had years ago when there was nothing more important to worry about than chores to do in the morning or outfits to wear to parties.

* * *

"Stars are awfully pretty tonight," Marshall said that evening, leaning back against his hands on the floor of her wooden porch.

They were sitting side by side on an old quilt of Millicent's, eating a batch of Chrissie's molasses cookies that she had brought out to share.

"Yes, they are," Millicent agreed, taking in the vast sky above them.

"Some nights, this just seems like the perfect thing to do . . ." Marshall said, his voice drifting off.

She knew exactly what he meant. It was so peaceful at that moment . . . and the sky so lovely. Being so high up, sometimes it was easy to forget how different the sky had looked back in St. Louis when she was young . . . but nights like this brought it all back, tenfold. The sky was clear, and the stars twinkled so bright above them that it looked as if your arm was long enough to reach out and pluck one from the sky. They twinkled and glowed at her, taunting her just to try. It was mesmerizing.

Marshall cast a look in her direction before gazing back up in the sky again. "I'm glad you didn't mind me taking you out here. I just needed someone to talk to . . . like we used to do before we grew up . . ."

Once again, Millicent knew his feelings. While George had acted as her big brother for so long, Marshall had always been her confidant, someone who felt things deeply, like she did. He knew how to listen and how to share the silence.

Of course, their relationship had changed when he had gotten interested in girls, and the things that he wanted to do with them. His new feelings hadn't set well with her, and she'd let him know it in no uncertain terms. Inevitably, Millicent's disapproval of his actions had interfered with his quest for female companionship of another kind. He stopped coming around to visit with her.

And before she knew it, a few years ago their quiet evenings had suddenly become a thing of the past.

"Kind of a strange day, huh?" Marshall asked, breaking the silence. His manner was tentative, strained. So unlike him.

She hid a smile. "Yes, it was."

"All of those women . . ."

"All of those picnic baskets!"

Marshall laughed. "I never saw so much fried chicken in my life."

"I'm certain Chrissie has the only living flock in town."

"Did you ever eat anything?"

"Do you ask because I came so noticeably empty-handed?"

"I did offer to share," Marshall corrected.

"Over Hannah Parson's dead body!"

He chuckled. "She sure didn't look in any hurry to share, did she? I tried to tell her that there was only so much good food a man could eat in one sitting."

Millicent smiled in spite of herself. "You sure tried, didn't you?"

"I did. Patsy James's potato salad is truly worth thinking about twice."

"At least some of the women let you bring the food home with you . . ."

"And I brought some of that to you."

"Oh, Marshall, did you really?" Millicent eyed the basket

he had deposited on her stoop with glee. It truly was a shame she'd never developed a knack for cooking.

"You want some now?"

"No, I already had some dinner. But thank you."

They sat in silence for a while, each lost in their own thoughts . . . Millicent imagining what would have occurred if she had happened upon Marshall alone in the field that afternoon. Would she have sat with him? Would he have wanted her to?

The night was curiously still. Only a faint birdcall reverberated in the distance. Millicent leaned back against her hands and stretched out her legs in front of her, glad for the comfort of the old quilt.

"Do you ever think about how things are?" Marshall's words seemed to startle the air, a few birds chirped, a frog croaked in irritation.

"What do you mean?"

"I mean, here we are, in Rocky River . . ."

She smiled at his proclamation. "We are that."

"Both trying to scratch out a living."

She chuckled at his words. She took in sewing, while he was the owner of a wildly successful saloon. "Some of us are scratching better than others."

"Millicent, honey, I'm serious."

So was she, thinking longingly of the things she'd had to do without. She forced herself to focus on his words.

"I'm sorry. What were you saying?"

"Is this . . . Rocky River and all, where you thought you'd end up?"

"Honestly, I don't know if I've ended up anywhere yet . . . but yes, ever since we moved here when I was a little girl, I felt like this was home."

His voice became quieter. "You never wished to leave, when your pa died . . ."

A sense of sadness washed over her. The feelings that she'd had, when everyone left after the funeral, and she was alone in the house for the first time came rushing back. Back then her whole future had seemed scary and dark. The house had felt too big, too empty.

She'd never imagined she would live alone; she'd always thought to have her own family by the time her father passed away. But his untimely death when she was twenty had changed all that. Little by little she'd had to come to terms with a life by herself . . . the memories still made her feel uncomfortable. Resolutely she pushed those dark thoughts away. "Where would I have gone, Marshall? And, to do what?"

"To live with relatives . . ."

"There are no relations that I'd want to reside with."

"You sure?"

"Marshall, they'd have me following their sets of rules, their way of doing things. It wouldn't be the way I'd want to live."

He didn't seem convinced. "But—"

"I'm fine. I don't have a lot of money, but I do all right. I take in my sewing, and of course I have what Pa left me, too."

"What will you do when you get married?"

Just hearing him say the word made Millicent shiver. "I don't know, actually. I guess what all married ladies do: raise children, keep house, try to be a good wife."

"But you haven't been in a hurry?"

She shrugged. "No . . ."

"No one special?"

She cast an uncertain glance in his direction. "Not who's taken me out. Not yet, anyway."

They sat in silence for a long spell, Marshall seeming to take her words seriously. "How will you know, do you think, when you find the right mate?"

"I'll know."

He chuckled at her tone. "Millicent, I'm serious. How will you know when you've found your man?"

Sitting up, she turned to face him. Did she dare answer him truthfully?

Of course not, she admonished herself. One did not tell the man of one's dreams that he was her one and only!

Um, not yet, at least. Thankful for the dim light, she whispered. "Because I won't want to be with anyone else, Marshall. I'll ache for his touch . . . I'll look forward to his briefest glances . . . I'll get dressed in the morning, with his appreciation in mind. That's how I'll know."

Something flickered in his expression. Millicent stared at him, hoping to see it again, but his face was once again thoughtful, composed.

"And until then?" he asked, his voice low and curiously gravelly.

She swallowed. "Until then, I'll wait."

The air seemed thicker suddenly. Millicent could feel the tension between them, thick and tangible. Mentally she cursed her tongue. What was she thinking, talking about aching for touches and getting dressed in the morning? Ladies just didn't speak of those things . . . and certainly not in mixed company! But then Marshall leaned toward her and she forgot to chastise herself further.

"Did you know that there's a part of me that was hoping

you were going to be at the picnic today . . . to be sitting, pretty as a picture on a quilt, basket in hand?"

Her mouth went dry. "No. Would you have sat with me?"

"I would have."

"You know my food would have been awful."

"It wouldn't have mattered."

She didn't know what to say to that.

Marshall stretched his arms then faced her a little more directly. "You've always been there for me . . . we've always had each other, haven't we?"

Where was he heading? Feeling that some kind of response was expected, she muttered, "Yes."

"I'm glad."

They sat for a while then, appreciating the evening, listening to the cicadas, enjoying the sense of comfort the other brought. Then Marshall leaned closer. Spoke again.

"Mill, until then . . . you gonna keep an open mind?"

That pine and tobacco scent wafted toward her again. She closed her eyes and breathed deep. "About what?"

"About the one?" he murmured. He shifted position to one hip and then brought his left hand to cup her chin gently.

He smelled of something else, too. Bay rum? Mint? She felt so lightheaded, she couldn't tell. She swallowed hard as his fingers traced the line of her throat.

"Millicent . . . on your Saturday dates . . ."

"Yes?"

His breath was warm as he leaned closer still. Her shoulders brushed his own. "Do you let those men kiss you good-night?"

She shook her head no.

His hand had made it down to her collarbone, his fingers tracing the ridge at the edge of her dress. "Has anyone kissed you good-night before?" His words were slow, measured, exactly like his touch.

Millicent was incapable of speaking. She shook her head no once more.

Marshall sighed, shifted again. Then she felt both hands curve around her ribs, inches from the rise of her breasts, and they slid so slowly, so gently. . . . His lips lowered and pressed against her cheek.

She exhaled abruptly, reminding herself to breathe. "Millicent, I would be honored," Marshall said quietly, "if I could be your first."

He waited only a fraction of an instant before finally claiming her mouth. Stunned, she felt his lips pass against her softly, then pass again, with more pressure this time.

This was exactly what she had dreamed of! Marshall, kissing her, with his arms around her body, holding her close. "Mar—" she began as she raised her hands to his chest, and felt his heart beat fast.

But he cut off her words. "Shh, darlin'," he murmured before kissing her again. And their kiss deepened, and Millicent tasted him, and felt his hand against the back of her head, pressing her closer, murmuring sweet words, heat radiating from him.

She held on for dear life. Never had she thought such a simple kiss could be like this! But her eyes opened then with the realization that Marshall's kisses were anything but simple. They were self-assured, and mature, and passionate. And slow, as if he had all the time in the world to hold her in his arms.

Never had she expected to feel dizzy and hot and out of

breath, all at the same time. Her hands gripped Marshall's shirt as he raised his head slowly. She glanced at his face. His eyes were closed, and he wore an expression that one might describe as reverent if they had been sitting in church. But then he bent down, her own eyes drifted shut, and they began again.

He sprinkled kisses on her cheek, her neck, on that place under her ear that no one had ever told her was sensitive. His hands lowered to circle her waist, then one drifted upwards, and cupped the back of her head gently. "Oh darlin'," he murmured again.

But when his hand began to carefully remove the pins in her hair, when she felt the heavy mass about to cascade down her back, Millicent started. "Marshall," she said, surprised.

He raised his head, his eyes cloudy in the moonlight. "Millicent, sweetheart . . ."

Oh, if only they were really in love right now! If only she'd heard words from him promising a future, of wedded bliss . . . of everything she had dreamed of!

But she hadn't.

Carefully she opened her eyes and peeked to see how he looked. He had a look in his eyes she wasn't all too comfortable with. They were knowing, and languid, and full of plans she knew she shouldn't be part of . . . yet. "Marshall," she said again, with more force, pressing against him. "We must stop. This isn't right."

His eyes focused. He stared at her in surprise, then he dropped both hands to the quilt as if she was suddenly on fire. "Beg pardon, Millicent," he said roughly as he moved a full six inches from her person. "I don't know what came over me."

Millicent bit her lip to fight the sudden chill that appeared. She didn't know what to say.

His eyes searched her face, and gently he took her hands in his. "You okay?"

She nodded, feeling bereft of his attentions, but knowing that she couldn't afford to encourage them. "Are you?"

The corners of his lips curved upward as he raked a hand through his hair. "Yes, ma'am, I am." He waited two beats, then added, "You are wonderful to kiss, Millicent."

There were so many ways she could have replied. Ways that she should have replied. Tartly, or teasing him . . . but it only seemed natural just to say what was utmost on her mind. "You are wonderful, too, Marshall."

"Next Saturday night . . ."

She turned her head. "Yes?"

"You busy?"

Of course she was! She always had a date scheduled, he knew that. "No . . ."

"Millicent, may I take you out?"

What could she say? "Yes."

He breathed deeply then, as if striving for a better control over himself, and stood up. "Well, then, I'll look forward to it."

She merely folded her legs under her arms and watched him pick up his hat.

When he straightened, their eyes met, and Millicent once again became lost in his gaze—the look that he gave her for a moment was raw and new.

He coughed. "I think I'll be leaving you now . . . I think that would be best," he murmured.

"All right."

Then he turned to walk away before once again facing her again. "Millicent . . ."

She lay her head on her knees. "Yes?"

"You, um, look lovely in the moonlight," he blurted.

She couldn't help but smile. "Thank you, Marshall."

He nodded briefly then turned and walked away.

Chapter Nine

Afew days later found Marshall in his office, ruminating about the state of his life.

Fact was, things just weren't going as planned. When he had set out to find the author of the letter, it had seemed so easy. Making up a list of prospective brides had been a pleasant endeavor as well. But irritating experiences were now far outnumbering the enjoyable ones. These days he was surrounded by people he scarcely recognized.

Confound it, there were just too many dishonest women in Rocky River! And there was just a whole slew of good-for-nothing men who had found a new lease on life by betting on his business, Marshall realized with dismay. Added to the mess was one certain woman, a lady who he had always been fond of in the most friendly way, who had gone and turned tables on him.

Thinking back to the antics at the picnic, he scowled. How could he have guessed that so many women would have pretended to write him a love note? How could he have foreseen that the average working man in town would have a vested interest in the outcome of his courting status?

And who had ever imagined that Millicent would press herself against him, and be so soft and sweet and so completely responsive?

Not him.

Marshall scratched his head in dismay. He had thought Millicent Drovers to be stand-offish type of girl, himself. Who would have guessed that her figure would be so soft? That those lips of hers, so giving, that those blue eyes up close, would have so many shades? It was enough to make a man recite times tables in order to keep a handle on himself.

And confound it if he didn't now have an even more legitimate reason to make sure that Edmund Baxter kept his stinkin' hands off her.

Weakly he recalled how he spent his time just five mere days ago. He had concentrated on business, on ordering new cases of whiskey, on George's new reasons about waiting to propose to Chrissie. Now everything was so twisted and strange. It left a bad taste in his mouth.

Somehow he had gotten himself in the middle of a mess of unwelcome situations and he needed to get out of them, fast.

But then Sadie came knocking on his door and things just got worse.

"Marshall," she called before barging on in like she always did.

He almost welcomed the interruption. "Yeah, Sadie? Everything going all right downstairs?"

She shifted uncomfortably. "That would be a matter of opinion."

"What's going on?"

"There's quite a few men wanting to speak with you."

"Is that right?" he asked, standing up and straightening his vest then donning his jacket. "Who's here?"

"Mr. Thomas and Mr. Jacobs, to begin with."

Surprise made him stop in his tracks. "Thomas and Jacobs?" Both men were upstanding citizens in the town. It was a surprise to imagine them frequenting the Dark Horse during the day.

Sadie screwed up her face. "They're looking pretty eager to see you."

As Marshall stepped out into the hallway, he grimaced as he heard the banker's voice in the din. "You better just go ahead and tell me what you know, Sadie. It would save us both a heap of trouble."

"Well, Marshall . . . ," she began slowly, like they had all the time in the world to stand in the hallway.

"Quick-like, okay?"

She sighed deeply. "Well, it's ah, like this. Edmund Baxter made a point of telling some of the menfolk 'round here that you were looking for a bride."

"He what?"

Sadie swallowed. "It gets worse. He also happened to let the men believe that you might be playing with all those picnicking girls' emotions."

Marshall stopped in his tracks. "And they believed him?"

Sadie chewed on her lip and gave him a world-weary look. "Marshall, there's no accounting for what men choose to believe of their daughters," she responded cryptically.

Sadie's final words rang in his ears as he came into view and saw seven of the town's more illustrious citizens decorating his barstools. "Gentlemen, it's a pleasure to have you here at the Dark Horse."

"Save us the greetings, Marshall," William Thomas, the town's banker, snapped. "We want to know what your intentions are toward our daughters."

"Intentions?" Quickly Marshall tried to recall if he had done anything untoward them, but the previous day's events were a jumbled heap in his mind.

"You heard me," Mr. Thomas said, his brows almost touching as he scowled.

Marshall was struck by how even a group of well-dressed gents could look like a mob. "Maybe we could sit down and discuss this?"

Eddie Jacobs, owner of the funeral parlor, spoke up first. "Rumor has it, Marshall, that some of our daughters' names are actually on betting lists that originated in this very establishment."

It was surely best to play dumb. "Where did you hear such a thing?"

"Edmund Baxter for one."

"I wouldn't cotton too much in what he says, now, Eddie," Marshall said warily.

"I wouldn't but for the fact that I just happened to overhear George Pepperal discuss this list as well."

"George?"

"Yep, he said there was quite some talk about this list of yours," William Thomas said testily. " 'Course, I could forget a lot about it if my daughter wasn't so all fired up about you."

"Pardon me?"

"I'm talking about this picnic you hosted. Here my Alyson thought she was your chosen one, and she minded something terribly about being one of twelve on that lawn."

"Now, wait a minute. Alyson cannot be blaming the picnic on me," Marshall corrected. "All I said was that I would meet the author of that note. It's not my fault that so many women don't recall whether they wrote me a note or not."

Eddie Jacobs spoke then. "Well Anna Jane, for that matter, says that she did not write you a note . . . she just couldn't resist the opportunity."

"I have a feeling that my Alyson was feeling the same way," William harrumphed. "Tell us, Marshall—when are you planning to set your date?"

Things were getting odder by the minute. "Date?"

"To choose your bride?"

"I haven't set one."

"Now, that don't seem quite fair," Eddie said. "Stringing these women on for an undisclosed amount of time . . ."

"Now listen, I ain't been stringing anyone along . . ."

"I think June ought to do it."

"How 'bout June fifteenth?"

He was sure he was choking. "Married in June?"

William nodded. "Now, that has a good ring to it, son. My wife will be pleased to know that we had this conversation. Good luck."

All the men looked happy with the outcome of the conversation and clapped him on the back on their way back to work.

Marshall felt around for a chair. Sadie pulled one out for him and eyed him with a withering expression. He sank down in relief.

Glancing up, he said, "Well, that went well, now didn't it?"

"Well for who?"

Marshall grimaced. "I don't know how in tarnation things got so danged twisted 'round here."

Sadie's brows went up as she pulled over a chair for herself. "Boss, you just don't get it, do you?" she asked, exasperated. "People have spring fever in Rocky River. They're interested in love notes and Sunday picnics right now like no other time of the year."

He didn't care for her explanation. "Spring fever?"

Sadie nodded sagely. "That's right. The snow is thawing, the air has a hint of warmth in it, the sky is as blue as a bluebonnet."

He quirked an eyebrow at that. "Blue as a bluebonnet?"

Sadie just snapped her fingers. "I know what I'm speaking of. Why, just yesterday morning my Will brought me a bouquet of wildflowers from the field near the mine. Love is in the air, Boss."

"Just because other people are in love doesn't mean they have to interfere with my private business."

"Your private business is one of the most interestin' things going on right now. You're just going to have to realize that the inordinate interest in your picnicking partners is just an unfortunate side effect to the fever."

Marshall groaned. "Sadie—"

"Don't worry, Boss. Come summer, things will cool off considerably. It will be too hot for love then."

Summer seemed like an eternity away. "Well, what do you think I should do in the meantime?"

Sadie crossed her arms over her chest, "I'd say you best go about finding a bride like you were planning to, Marshall Bond. Time's a-wastin'."

"Thanks for that sage advice, Sadie."

She didn't catch his sarcasm. Pulling a worn cloth from the pocket on her apron, she merely grunted. "Anytime, Boss, anytime."

Chapter Ten

Things weren't going a whole lot better for Millicent. Still caught off guard by her embrace with Marshall, she was late with her appointment with Mrs. Anderson and barely made it to town to pick up her order of supplies before sundown.

But all of that paled compared to the appearance of Edmund Baxter on her doorstep.

"Mr. Baxter," she uttered in surprise when she answered the door, realizing that he just might be the most unwelcome person to ever grace her doorstep.

If he noticed her reluctance to allow him entrance, he gave no indication. He only nodded his head slightly and gave her a small leer. "Miss Millicent."

As she glanced at his smarmy expression, she swallowed hard. Though she couldn't explain it, there was something about him that frightened her, in a way that not even the most disreputable miner or cowhand did. Perhaps it was his size, or his age, his lack of teeth . . . or his constant smirk? "This is quite a surprise," she said uncomfortably.

He only stared back at her. Millicent was aware of the many times she had rebuffed his offers of courting. She gripped the door frame and tried to look composed.

"Miss Millicent, may I come in?"

Oh dear. Just the thought of being alone with him made her uneasy. "Would you care to sit on the front porch? The day is rather mild."

He looked as if he wanted to do anything but. However, after a moment's pause, he replied easily enough. "Thank you, ma'am."

He sat down on the proffered swing and Millicent had no choice but to gingerly sit beside him. They sat in silence for a few minutes before he spoke.

"I imagine that you've heard of the disgraceful conduct of Marshall Bond," he said without preamble.

Immediately she relaxed. Perhaps Edmund was just looking to share some gossip. "Disgraceful?"

"I'll have you know that he has ludicrously begun a betting pool for prospective brides."

Millicent gripped her hands together. What to do? Ladies weren't supposed to know about such saloon gossip . . . but she also felt compelled to defend Marshall. "I did hear about that, actually."

Edmund clasped his hands in front of him tightly. "I, for one, am appalled by such behavior."

Millicent had to school her face into a most serious expression. After all, what could she say to a man who had suddenly developed manners with the onslaught of gold? The irony was certainly hard to ignore. Land sakes, only a few years ago, everyone was trying to convince the man to bathe regularly! "What does Marshall's actions have to do with you or I?"

He looked momentarily disconcerted to be asked such a direct question. "I'm afraid that your name is on this list."

Again she forced herself to appear only mildly interested. "Yes?"

He gave her a sideways look. "Doesn't this news bother you?"

Millicent shrugged. "Last I heard, a woman still had some say in her choice of groom. I don't see how Marshall's actions will affect me, one way or another."

"I saw him walk you home the other night."

Goodness. Millicent hoped that was all he had seen! "He did do that."

He lowered his voice and looked as if he was about to scoot closer. Millicent forced herself to sit rigid. "If your father was alive, I'm sure he would want you to stay as far away from this gossip as possible, Miss Millicent. If you're not careful, your reputation will suffer."

The unspoken implication was clear. Her sparkling reputation was the only thing she truly had to recommend her. "I believe you're right, Edmund. My father would demand that I strive to be above such talk."

"That's why I'm proposing that you end this ridiculous preoccupation with Saturday night dates and pick someone to squire you full time," he said slowly, with a hint of satisfaction in his voice. "Someone who you feel that you could have a future with. Someone older. Experienced."

Oh, my. Millicent couldn't help but stare at the older man in shock. "You came over here to warn me off from Marshall Bond's attentions?"

"No. I came here to let you know that one day soon you

might find yourself in the middle of some wicked gossip . . . if you don't change your ways."

Was he blackmailing her? Telling her in no uncertain terms that if she didn't finally succumb to his advances that she would have to fear for her reputation? "But . . ."

"Miss Millicent, my motives are honorable."

He positively was leering at her now. Leering right through the lock of blond hair that hung limply over his left eye. Oh dear. Cautiously she attempted to scoot away from him. "Mr. Baxter . . ."

"I came over here to offer my attentions to you, in the best sense of the word." He leaned closer.

She caught the whiff of stale whiskey and an underlying scent of mud and red clay. But over all of that was an overwhelming odor of cheap cologne, the kind that was only sold by the peddler who came in the summer months. The smell was sweet, and clinging, just like the scent of over-ripened fruit. Millicent coughed delicately. "I don't desire your attentions, sir."

"You just don't know what you desire, ma'am," Edmund said with force, then leaned forward to kiss her.

Millicent stared wide-eyed at Edmund and then gasped as it looked as if he was about to plant his thin lips right upon hers, without so much as a by-your-leave! "Mr. Baxter!" she exclaimed as she scrambled off the seat, leaving him grasping the sides for support as it swayed drunkenly.

He scowled at her. "Millicent, I'm not asking for more from you than what you've given your other beaus."

"I have not shared my kisses with my beaus," she said indignantly, and even stamped her foot for good measure.

His expression darkened. "Are you saying that you have

never, ever let a man touch those lips of yours?" he sneered.

Startled, she pressed her fingers to her mouth and shook her head.

His eyes glittered. "Come now. I can scarce believe that. There must be more of an attraction to your evenings than just your scintillating conversation."

Millicent stared at him in shock, knowing that he was insinuating that she was lacking in a myriad of ways. However, it was the look in his eyes, together with the tone of his voice, that made her catch her breath.

Suddenly she wished for the comfort of her father, the security of a family . . . she felt completely, totally alone in the world, bereft like she hadn't for several years. Summoning every once of courage, she placed a hand on her hip and attempted look as foreboding as she was able. "Mr. Baxter, the answers to those questions are certainly none of your business."

"I don't see why," he said glaring at her coldly. "Here I am, offering myself to your future happiness."

"I'll try to survive on my own."

"Survive?" he uttered with disdain.

She said nothing.

His eyebrows lowered and he stood up. "The problem with you, Miss Millicent, is that you're a mite too high in the instep. You need someone to take you down a notch or two. Teach you how to mind."

Then he stepped forward. A shiver of fear trickled through her, her body suddenly felt damp and worn out, as if she had run a race in the middle of July. "Mr. Baxter, it is time for you to leave," she said as firmly as she was able.

He smacked his hand against his thigh, the sound reverberating though the confines of the porch. Millicent winced in fear. "It is high time you learned a lesson," he snapped, stepping closer. "I swear by all that's mighty that—"

But he was prevented from finishing that thought by the appearance of Chrissie. "Millicent, I'm so glad you're here," she exclaimed loud enough for the whole street to hear.

Millicent sagged in relief as Chrissie scampered up the front steps and looped an arm through her own. "Chrissie, thank goodness," she murmured.

"I was just telling Pa that we ought to visit you for a moment, perhaps have a glass of tea," Chrissie said brightly.

"Your pa is on the way?"

"Yes he is," Chrissie said, eying Edmund defiantly. "As a matter of fact, we should hear him arriving at any moment."

Edmund stared icily at Chrissie for one long moment then turned to Millicent. "This isn't over, Miss Drovers, not by a long shot."

"Good evening, Mr. Baxter," she said as firmly as her shaking voice would allow.

Chrissie merely just stared at him, then guided Millicent back into her house.

Once inside, Millicent sank down into her couch with relief. "Oh, Chrissie, I just don't know what I would have done if you hadn't shown up. He was so mad."

She patted her shoulder. "I know, dear. My daddy saw him come your way, and figured it was trouble."

"Is your pa really stopping by?"

The brief knock on the door answered that. Chrissie stood up to let her tall father in. "Oh, Daddy," she gasped, grabbing his arm and pulling him into Millicent's small living room. "I'm so glad we came over. That Edmund Baxter was truly upsetting Millicent."

Mr. McKenna patted Chrissie's head then turned to her. Concern etched his expression. "Did he harm you, Milly?"

She couldn't help it, she began to shake. The enormity of what almost happened was fierce in her mind. "No, thank goodness, just threatened me."

Chrissie's father, a big man, who many likened to Paul Bunyan behind his back, knelt in front of her. "What did he say?"

She bit her lip to keep the tears from falling. "I'm not really sure," she said wearily. "I think he wants me to marry him . . . he was trying to kiss me . . . and he's upset about Marshall's list."

Anton McKenna shared a knowing look with his daughter. "Did Marshall know Edmund was going to come pay you a call today?"

"Goodness, I don't know. I doubt it." She glanced at her best friend. "Chrissie?"

Chrissie knelt down beside her pa, took her hand in her own. "I'm sure he didn't, Mill. That Edmund Baxter only skulks around the edges of this town. He never does anything straight out."

"All I can say was that I certainly did not expect Edmund Baxter to pay me a call this evening." Finally her voice cracked. "Oh, Mr. McKenna, what am I going to do?"

Mr. McKenna merely leaned forward and pressed a gentle kiss to her forehead in response. "Don't you worry, Milly. I'll take care of everything." He stood up then. "Chrissie, would you be willing to stay here for a spell? I have some business that needs attending to down the road."

Chrissie's eyes widened. "Of course I'll stay here for a while." Then she turned to her dear friend. "Millicent, how 'bout I help you with Mrs. Anderson's dresses?"

Although she knew exactly what was behind Chrissie's motivation, Millicent was too shaken to ignore her friend's kind gesture. "I'd love the help, thank you."

"I'll be back in about an hour, girls," Anton McKenna said quietly, then walked out of Millicent's home, as quickly as he had come.

Chapter Eleven

Marshall looked up from his paper when Anton Mc-Kenna rapped on the door, then immediately stood up as soon as he saw the other man's expression. "What's up, Anton? Trouble in town?"

"Trouble with Baxter."

"How so?"

"Paid a call on Millicent this evening."

A cold chill coursed through him. "What happened?" he asked, already grabbing his coat and preparing to leave.

Anton held out a hand. "Now, hold on, son. Chrissie and I got there before much harm was done."

Much harm? Marshall could only see red. "That no-good snake is going to rue the day he began trying to force himself on innocent women."

"I agree, Marshall," Anton said quietly. "Sit down. You need to hear the whole story before you go running off half-cocked."

"Anton . . ."

"Millicent is just fine. Chrissie's with her, and they're sewing dresses."

"But—"

"You would have been proud of that girl. From what I could tell, Miss Millicent held her own against him."

"She shouldn't be having to. Baxter has no business forcing his attentions on her. He'll know that better when I get through with him."

"Marshall, you need to steady yourself. This isn't the way to go about making an impact," the elder man said steadily.

"What do you think I should do? Just sit here?"

"No, I think you should go beat the tar out of him . . . but that's not the best course to take."

"What is, do you suppose?"

"I think you should let a couple of us go visit him with you."

"What? You don't think I can handle this on my own?"

"I think you can, son, but Baxter has a way of stretching the truth and twisting situations. If there's more than just one or two of us, then he won't be so predisposed to change the facts, if you will."

What Anton McKenna said made sense. "How soon can you round these men up, do you think?"

Anton strode to the door. "Give me five minutes."

And with that, the older man left Marshall alone with only his thoughts for company.

Eight men had decided to join Marshall and Anton, George one of them. In addition, several had already seen Edmund at the Scarlet Lady, shooting off his mouth and drinking shots of whiskey.

They entered the saloon and Marshall was struck by how different one drinking establishment could be from another.

The Scarlet was dirty and a foul smell hung in the room, a peculiar combination of unwashed bodies and lye soap. The mixture was pungent and offensive.

The Scarlet was not a favored place of anyone . . . not the worn-looking bargirls, with their painted faces and too-easy smiles, not the miners who were down on their luck and spending their family's bread money. Simply put, it was the last stop for many people. Despair filled the air.

Which was why Edmund Baxter looked even more out of place than usual. He was dressed to the hilt, clad in a shiny shirt and too-tight pants. His hat was a Stetson, and far too fancy for the likes of Rocky River.

He glanced up when the band of men strolled in, then immediately produced a sneer.

"Slumming, Marshall?"

His fist tightened. "Hardly."

Anton stepped forward. "Hear you've been making some social calls in your spare time."

Edmund scowled. "What, your daughter been telling you lies again?"

Once again, his sharp words had found a target. Anton looked about ready to forget everything he'd said to Marshall and just belt him one.

George looked at both, sighed, and then took his turn. "You best watch your mouth, Baxter."

Edmund glanced at him in surprise, and Marshall understood the man's surprise. George was the most affable fellow in town. He got along with most everyone, and managed to always stay away from confrontations.

"It's like this, Edmund," George continued as he pulled

up a chair and sat next to him. "When Miss Millicent's pa died . . . he was trapped in the shaft for a good ten minutes, knowing that there was nothing nobody could do for him. His leg had been broken and a layer of rocks had landed on his chest when the ceiling had given way. Robert Drovers was bleeding terribly, but had some things that he needed to say, before he ran out of time. Everybody who was there knew the same thing. Mr. Drovers began to talk, and everyone else just listened." George paused for a moment, eyed Edmund to see if he understood that he was talking about a dying man's last words. For once Edmund's expression was solemn.

George continued. "He talked about his dreams, and his wife who had died years ago, and his sweet Millicent. And he extracted promises from a whole slew of men that they'd look out for her, make sure she'd be okay."

Marshall stood, dumbfounded. Why had he never known this?

George continued. "My pa was down there with him. So was Mr. McKenna, and Mr. Thomas, too, for that matter."

Marshall looked at the group of men. Each wore a stony expression, as if the words that had been spoken by Robert Drovers had just been said yesterday. No wonder Anton knew that this would be the right thing to do.

"Each man promised that he'd look out for Millicent," Anton McKenna said quietly. "Every man said that they'd make sure she became the lady that her mother would have wanted her to be, that Mr. Drovers would have never been able to do by himself."

"And people did just that," Mr. Thomas murmured, steel in his tone. "People treated her kindly. Put her on a pedestal. Gave her their time . . . let her know that although her family was gone, she wasn't alone."

Edmund scowled. "So?"

"So, we're just telling you that you made a mistake," George said.

"I . . ."

"There's nothing to say," Anton McKenna said harshly. "You shouldn't have been anywhere near Millicent."

Edmund stared at Marshall with disdain. "I am not the one who's been ruining her reputation. I haven't been taking her out in the middle of the evening."

Marshall gritted his teeth. "If you're referring to myself, you better believe that I have nothing but the highest regard for Millicent."

"I do to," Edmund whined. "I asked her to marry me this evening. What have you done, Marshall?"

Suddenly, Marshall found the eyes of ten men focused on him. "I don't need to do anything for her. I've been her friend for years."

"And what have you ever offered her?"

"I've offered her friendship and care."

"And?"

"And I'm escorting her out this Saturday night," he finished weakly. "But you are not going to go anywhere near her again, do you understand me? She is too good for the likes of you!"

A thick eyebrow rose at his words. "For you too, boy."

In spite of himself, Marshall could feel his neck heat. Edmund Baxter was absolutely right. Millicent deserved more than a future beside a saloon owner, especially given the fact that her pa had asked so many upstanding citizens in the town to look out for her. "I know that she is," he said simply, then turned to the rest of the men.

George stared back at him, his expression telling Marshall that he was getting it all wrong. But Marshall wasn't ready to figure out what was right . . . at least not right there, in front of all of the men. "I'm going to Millicent, to make sure that she's all right, to offer my assistance," he said simply. "Thank you for coming."

And with that, he sauntered out, past the dirty tables, past the bargirl in the faded red dress.

"Marshall?" She said his name hesitantly, quietly.

He turned to the voice. The woman in the dress shifted her weight to one hip, the other jutted out in invitation. "I'm not interested."

"I was hoping you might need some help at the Dark Horse?" Her words were rushed, breathless.

There was something in her tone that caused him to finally look directly at her. "Listen . . . we only serve drinks there, no favors."

Her voice lowered, became even more hesitant. "That's what I was hoping for."

Even in the dim light, Marshall could see that this woman was crying for help. She looked worn out and tired, and a faint bruise marred one heavily made-up cheek. Forcing his mind to concentrate on her, he said gently, "What's your name, honey?"

Her eyes were wary, afraid to hope. "Justine."

"Come on over about noon tomorrow. Wear a dress that covers you up. No makeup. Ask to speak to Sadie. We'll go from there."

"Thank you," she said, then stepped forward. "About Edmund Baxter . . . better be careful around him. He won't take this business today lightly. He's never been trouble, but he's kind of got a wild look about him tonight."

"I noticed that, too, Justine. Thanks."

And with that he tipped his hat to her and made his way out into the open air, breathing in the clean, brisk scent of the evening thankfully. Then he strode down the street, wondering what in the world he was going to tell Millicent.

Chapter Twelve

Marshall wasn't sure what he expected to see when he paid a call on Millicent, but he sure as fire wasn't expecting to see her chatting happily with Chrissie over a set of dresses. He'd let himself in after a brief knock, prepared to dry tears and make unlimited promises. He'd been ready to hold her close and promise protection, not sit on the sofa and listen to her chat about bustles.

Yes, Millicent's calm facade unnerved him, and Chrissie's knowing look just made him feel silly. All of his grand plans evaporated and he stood in Millicent's modest living room, feeling too big for the furniture and too gangly to move around.

"Good evening, Marshall," Chrissie greeted him.

He nodded his head. "Chrissie, Miss Millicent."

The only sign, as far as he could tell, that his presence affected Millicent was that her fingers stilled and she sat motionless.

Marshall cleared his throat. "I thought I'd come on by

90

and check on you, Mill. I saw Anton McKenna a few moments ago . . ." His voice drifted off.

Then her blue eyes met his and he found himself lost again. Suddenly he knew that she was frightened and needed comfort. Her eyes sparkled with unshed tears and dared him to step forward and take on her troubles. He couldn't resist.

Pulling up a ladder back chair near her, he reached out for a hand. "Millicent, you okay?"

"Yes," she answered so quietly it just broke his heart. Unsure what to say, Marshall glanced at Chrissie. Her lips were pursed and she gave him a look that told him directly that Millicent was a heap more affected than she was letting on.

When Millicent said nothing else, Chrissie cleared her throat. "Um, Marshall, so you saw my pa?"

"Yes I did. He filled me in on what happened this afternoon."

Millicent's hands clenched tighter.

Chrissie smoothed her skirts. "He on his way home?"

Remembering how he had left the man, Marshall nodded. "He should be 'round directly."

"I think, if you don't mind, Milly, that I'll just go outside and wait for him," Chrissie said, hopping up and already making her way to the door.

That seemed to break Millicent's reverie. She looked up and smiled wanly. "Um, all right, Chrissie. Thank you for coming over."

Chrissie waved a hand. "That's what friends are for, silly. I'm glad I did." Then, after pulling on her coat, she turned to them both. "I'll be seeing you tomorrow."

When they were alone, Marshall stood up. "How about

some tea?" He was ready to do anything to bring a smile to her lips again.

She looked at him curiously. "You know how to make that?"

"Ma'am, you're looking at a saloon owner. I believe I can take care of most any type of beverage."

"Oh, well, I'd like tea, thank you."

When Marshall went into her little kitchen, Millicent finally let her head fall back against the back of the chair. She felt exhausted and dirty, even though Edmund really hadn't done anything to warrant those feelings.

However, for once she was in no hurry to pin up a facade and pretend that she felt fine. Her close call with Edmund reminded her of just how vulnerable she was, living alone. Wearily she realized that she'd been living in a fantasy world, expecting all men who called on her to be gentlemen. It was time she left that place and entered reality. Goodness, she lived in a mining town, for goodness sakes, not Boston!

For the first time in months, the loss of her father felt terrible and unfair. Why did she have to lose both parents so young? Why had she been forced to grow up so quickly?

Marshall's appearance, holding a delicate china teacup with pink flowers painted on it made her smile. He held it with care, and handed it to her before sitting next to her on the sofa.

"So, what happened?" he asked quietly, after she had a few fortifying sips. Millicent needed no reminder to what he was referring.

She shrugged. "Oh, Marshall. Edmund came calling. He

was making accusations about my character, about my Saturday night dates."

"And . . ."

"He made insinuations that perhaps those dates hadn't been as chaste as I'd led people to believe."

Marshall's eyes turned flinty. "And then?"

"He started talking about you and me, about how he knew I'd been in your company the other night. Marshall, it was if he'd been spying on me, and knew that we kissed!" To her mortification, she could feel the tears once again well up in her eyes. She held out to her hand to him and squeezed it tightly.

"Millicent, even if he had seen us, which I doubt, we did nothing to be ashamed of."

"But we shouldn't have done anything."

"Honey, I'm not going to let you turn a simple kiss, something that was sweet and dear, into something to be ashamed of."

"It didn't feel that way when Edmund said it," she admitted. "I felt embarrassed and discomfited that he knew I wasn't quite as proper as I led everyone to believe. And he's right . . . I do know better. All I have is my reputation, Marshall."

Marshall leaned back against her little couch, his mouth set in a fine line. "Well, what happened next?"

"He tried to kiss me." She glanced at Marshall to gauge his reaction. "I told him no . . . but he kept saying that I needed an older man, someone to take care of me, someone to keep me in line."

The hand that held hers tightened. Marshall stared at the wall behind her for a moment, then met her gaze. "Then Mr. McKenna came?"

"Well, first Chrissie arrived, then Mr. McKenna, who had a few words for him. Edmund wasn't happy, but he left easily enough."

He rubbed his thumb over her hand. "I'm sorry I wasn't here earlier."

"You couldn't have been expected sooner, Marshall. You didn't know that he was going to come by."

"I know, but all the same, I wish I had been."

She smiled weakly. "Well, it's all over with now." She picked up her tea again and took a few more nourishing sips. "You make a fine cup of tea, Mr. Bond," she teased, attempting to lighten the mood.

His eyes sparkled. "Thank you kindly." He leaned back then, stretched his legs out in front of him. "We still on for our date Saturday night?"

"I don't know . . ."

"I hope so. I still have that whole issue of the love letter, you know."

Guilt pierced her consciousness. Here Marshall was, so eager to defend her honor, and she'd been lying to him for the last few weeks! She truly needed to tell him the truth. It wasn't fair for her to lead him on, especially when he'd been such a good friend to her.

But in spite of her good intentions, she nodded. "I'm looking forward to the opera, and your company, of course."

"I am, also." He glanced out the window. Twilight was turning to night. Already the first star had appeared.

Millicent knew he needed to leave. Not only was it not proper for him to be sitting in her living room at night, but he also had the Dark Horse. She imagined all of the goings on that were taking place there. Surely everyone was wondering where the owner had gone off to?

Perhaps he'd been thinking the same thing. Marshall stood up, reached for his hat. "Will you be okay? I should probably be leaving, but I can stay, if you need me."

"I'll be fine. I'm just going to get cleaned up and prepare for bed, anyway." Then a thought occurred to her. "Marshall, you don't think Edmund will come back tonight, do you?"

His look was shuttered, as if he knew something he wasn't going to share with her. "No, I don't believe he will." Then he stood up and reached for her hand. "Good evening, Millicent."

She stood up also. "Good-night, and thank you."

He pressed a kiss to her hand. "You're welcome, darlin'."

And then he walked out, putting on his hat as he went.

Millicent stood alone in the room. If she tried hard enough, she could smell the remnants of his scent in the air. It made her feel protected and safe.

Then she did something she could never in her life recall doing—she turned the lock in her door before going to bed.

No evidence of their emotional evening was apparent that Saturday night as Millicent sat next to Marshall in a lovely green dress. The tapered sleeves were threaded with gold strands, the fabric was silk, a small bustle gave her becoming curves, and the dress sported no less than twenty-three buttons.

It was a gown she'd made in her spare time, the year she was in mourning for her father. It had given her an outlook and a hint of what her future could be if she didn't give in to despair. She'd never had the courage to wear it out before, thinking it was too fine for just a Saturday night date. But as she smoothed her hands over the luxurious fabric, she felt very fine indeed.

Marshall, for his part, had on a purple brocade vest under his black jacket. He looked tempting and dazzling, and Millicent could scarcely keep her eyes off of his handsome presence.

Of course, his looks were not the only thing on her mind. She'd decided to tell him the truth, in the middle of the opera. That way he couldn't yell at her when she finally told him. Surely he wouldn't raise his voice to her in front of half the town? Mentally she practiced her speech. Perhaps she would be matter of fact; tell them that he'd been mistaken in his assumption, but she couldn't bear to correct him or perhaps hurt his feelings.

No, that wasn't quite right.

Maybe she should try for a silly, light-hearted mood. She could attempt to be chatty, perhaps begin the conversation by relaying that she knew of the funniest set of circumstances that had been happening around Rocky River. She pressed a hand to her lips. Goodness, how would he react to that? Would he think he was part of some secret trick?

"Millicent? Millicent are you enjoying yourself, darlin'?"

Startled, she turned to Marshall. He looked completely too at ease to suit herself. He wore a lazy smile and his bearing looked relaxed and loose. Almost as if he was play-acting just as much as the performers on stage. Privately she wondered if he didn't think much of opera.

"Yes, I am," she finally answered. "It's always a good night when they have a new show."

"What's the name of this one, again?"

"*The Marriage of Frank.*"

He looked confused. "Wasn't it *Marriage of Figaro*, or something?"

"Yes, but I believed they changed some parts of it to make it more appealing in Rocky River."

He leaned back in his seat, looking skeptical and disgruntled. "I see."

Oh, my. Did he frown upon play adaptations? Was Marshall one who was really fond of structure in his life, who didn't like any unnecessary changes? Would he be upset to find out that his life had changed for no real reason? Perhaps so.

She darted a look at him. He looked to be staring around the room, looking at all the people except for those on stage.

Goodness. Maybe she should strive for tears. She could cry prettily and beg his forgiveness. Although . . . would he see through her act and think less of her? Chewing on her lip, she considered. She imagined so. Hmmm. No, the right course would be to just say what was on her mind. She would just admit to the whole tale, and her reluctance to tell the truth because she'd secretly had a tendre for him for years.

Then it would be all out in the open, and she could sleep well at night.

Exactly.

Unbidden, she recalled a chat that she'd had with her mother, so long ago, when she hadn't wanted to drink a spoonful of castor oil. Her mama had said that some things were unpleasant in life, but they just had to be done.

This was one of those times.

"Marshall?" she whispered hesitantly.

Instantly he leaned down toward her. "Yes?"

"There's something that I need to tell you. It's kind of important."

He looked surprised. "Right here, during the play?"

"Yes, I believe so."

He looked worried, concerned.

Millicent shifted her hips, bought time by arranging the folds in her dress. "Well, it actually is of great magnitude."

His posture stiffened at her words. "All right . . ." He pulled his chair a little closer to her. His leg brushed against the voluminous folds of her dress. "I'm listening."

Oh, this was so hard! "Do you recall a couple of weeks ago, when you received that letter?"

He smiled. "A thing like that is kind of hard to forget."

"Yes, I imagine so."

"It's one of those life-changing experiences, I believe."

"Uh huh," she said weakly.

"Truth is, I don't know what I would have done with my life if I hadn't received it," Marshall continued, sounding more forthcoming than usual. "It's caused me to reevaluate my plans and realize that I need to plan my future."

A lump formed in her throat. Oh, how was she going to say this? "Well, um, that note was, ah . . ."

"What are you two doing, chatting so secret-like?" George asked to their left.

Millicent looked up in shock. "Why, Chrissie, George, I'm afraid I didn't see you approach."

George smiled knowingly. "I guess not. The play's been over a good four minutes. Haven't you noticed?"

She shook her head in wonder, then stood up. "Not at all." She glanced at Marshall. He was staring at her in wonder. She turned to George and Chrissie. "So, did y'all enjoy the show?"

Chrissie smiled becomingly, her blond curls bouncing as she turned her head to George. "Not as much as *Heaven*, though I can't think why. We're on our way to the hotel for a cup of coffee . . . would you care to join us?"

Marshall looked at Millicent for a long moment. "What would you like to do, Mill? Do you want to finish what you were telling me first?"

"No! I mean, my goodness, no. It was nothing important. Let's go get some coffee."

He looked at her skeptically. "All right, then, if that's what you want."

And with that, he took her arm and they made their way down the wooden stairs to the grand entry hall of the opera house. Before she knew it, Millicent was fielding questions about her gown and laughing with her friends about the play.

And if she felt the slightest twinge of guilt about still not telling Marshall the truth, why she didn't show it . . . not one bit.

Chapter Thirteen

However, she didn't feel the same way late the following evening. Her conscience pricked at her, and she knew that there was only one thing to do: write Marshall another note.

Well, write him a *letter*, she amended to herself. After all, she never actually written him a letter in the first place . . . that was the whole problem!

Still in her nightgown, she penned a letter. As clearly as possible, she tried to convey that his receipt of the first letter was completely an accident, and that he should forget all ideas about having a secret admirer.

However, she included with a feeling of self-righteousness, she should in no way feel responsible for his confusion of feelings. Most men would have come to the same conclusions. He should remember that he was still an admired man, and the author of the note held no hard feelings about his erroneous assumptions.

Millicent read over her work and nodded. So far it had

the perfect tone. Sympathetic to his plight, but clearly stating that she had no responsibility for his conclusions. Then for good measure, she added as a postscript:

For goodness sakes, you need to move on with your life! Turn the page in your book of life and begin a new chapter. Stop deluding yourself that you have a secret admirer.

And for good measure, Millicent signed the note, *A Concerned Friend*.

Feeling moderately better, the way she felt after doing an unpleasant chore, Millicent donned her wool cape and quickly made her way to Marshall's front door.

In the distance she heard boisterous activity. A shock of male laughter floated through the air, followed by feminine giggles. Once again Millicent was reminded that Rocky River was still a mining town, full of disreputable people who frequented the many drinking and gaming establishments that she was supposed to be unaware of.

However, on her street, all was quiet. She felt perfectly safe strolling down the street to deliver her missive.

The moon gave off a faint glow as she purposefully strode to Marshall's door, and set the note under a sturdy gray-colored rock, then just as quickly she made her way back home.

Yes, it was subterfuge, she admitted privately to herself as she entered her home again. Yes, she would have been better off just facing Marshall and telling him the truth. But she knew she wasn't able to do that. Surely this was the next best thing?

As she made her way up her stairs to her cozy bed, once again she recalled his kisses. In spite of herself, she began to hope. Perhaps this note would create some changes in her life, this time. Perhaps Marshall would come to his

senses and realize that other women just weren't for him . . .
that his heart only had a desire for Millicent Drovers.

Sleepily, she envisioned her future with Marshall. She
could tend to his needs in their cozy home . . . prepare him
coffee when he woke up after a busy night at the Dark
Horse. She'd be able to create a feminine emphasis in his
life. He'd look forward to geraniums and pansies adorning
his window boxes. Well, when he got window boxes, she
amended.

And they'd have children . . . and go to church together,
and the opera every now and then. And Marshall would
kiss her at night . . . and hold her in his strong arms, and
tell her that she was the most wonderful woman in the
world, that no other lady could hold a candle to her sweet
glow.

And they'd look back at these days and laugh, recogniz-
ing how foolish each was to hold what was certainly their
destiny at bay.

With a smile on her lips, Millicent fell asleep, sure that
the next day would bring an answer to her dreams.

Marshall wore the opposite expression the next morning
as he pulled the letter out from his vest pocket and stared
at it with suspicion. He had to admit that he'd been a little
taken aback when he found yet another note for him. But,
then, reevaluating his situation, he amended his thoughts.
Why, of course his admirer would be writing to him again.
After all, nothing had gone right with his plans . . . the picnic had ended up being a complete failure.

He imagined that his little letter-writer was feeling the
same way. She was probably at that picnic, wondering why
he was so confused. Hmm. And maybe she'd even heard

about his theater date with Millicent. That was sure to rile up an amorous lady's ire, without a doubt.

But when he tore open the seal, and then read what the inscription said, he let out a string of epithets that could only be heard in the depths of a mine, when an explosion seemed imminent.

Sadie, not one to cotton foul language in any establishment that she deemed to work at, came rushing over.

"Boss, what's wrong with you? I've was just telling Justine here that you were a good man to be workin' for. Now I gotta go amend my words."

"Sadie, do you know anything about this?" He waved the letter in front of her nose, like a rebel flag in battle.

"What is it?" She eyed it with a look of trepidation. "That one of your love letters?"

What did he call the thing? "I don't know. It's by the same woman who wrote the first one, but it's a little different in tone."

Sadie pulled up a chair next to him, her look instantly maternal. "Bad news?"

He shrugged. "I don't know what to call it. Surprising, maybe." He stared at the letter like it was a rattler about to bite him. "Sadie, go ask Justine to get George over here, would you?"

Glancing at the other occupants in the room, who were trying hard to look busy but were actually working hard at eavesdropping, she nodded. "Sure, Boss. I'll send her over to the mercantile right now."

After she left, Marshall fingered the note again, then breathed a sigh of relief when George approached not ten minutes later. "You gotta see this," he said simply as he pushed the offending note his friend's way.

George read it, looked at Marshall in shock, and then read it again. "Woo-whee! You got yourself into a heap of trouble."

"*I* got myself? You were right there, egging me on, telling me I had a justified love letter in the first place."

"I was only sharing my opinion."

Marshall narrowed his eyes.

George shifted in his chair a little. "Maybe they're not written by the same person? Word's gotten 'round town, about how you received a note under your rock and all . . . maybe it was written by a . . . ah . . . an impersonator."

Marshall's mood brightened. "You think so?"

He shook his head. "No. I'd know that curlicue 'T' anywhere. That note was written by the same person, no doubt."

Marshall felt like throwing the note at George. "I just can't believe it, George. I feel like nine-tenths of a fool. Here I was, going around, feeling irresistible, when all signs now say that I wasn't even invited anywhere."

George nodded solemnly. "Yep. You went and invited yourself to someone else's picnic."

"Did you see any girl there who looked disappointed, like she was expectin' someone else?"

"Hard to say, Marshall. All the girls looked disappointed to me. After all, there were at least a dozen of them and only one man."

"And those fathers," he added, scowling. "And the wedding in June!"

George nodded in agreement. "And the betting pool, too. Things are a real mess, that's a fact."

Marshall stared at the letter as he pulled out a cigar and lit it. "I'm just not sure what to do now."

"I'd say just go on with your life, pick a bride, and thank fate for setting you in the marrying direction. Just like the note said."

"The note said for me 'to turn the page'! I'm not about to begin taking advice about my life from some cowardly woman who is too timid to even sign her God-given name!"

George waited a full minute before replying. "But, Marshall, you were all fired up to get a life's mate. That's what you wanted, right?"

Somehow getting married didn't have the same appeal as it did when he thought he was an object of attention. "I guess. I don't know . . . I'm just in a real quandary."

Just then they were joined by Sadie, carrying a bottle of whiskey as well as a strong-smelling cup of coffee.

"What are you doing, Sadie?" Marshall asked. "I didn't ask for that."

Sadie just set the coffee down in front of him and poured a liberal dose of whiskey into a shot glass. "You're gonna need this in a minute."

George looked askance. "What happened? Something wrong?"

Sadie sighed heavily.

"Come on, Sadie. Spit it out," Marshall said. "What happened?"

"Only that someone saw your letter-writing sweetheart deliver your letter last night, and the word's all over town."

"Say again?"

Sadie helped herself to a chair. "You heard me right," she said, tapping her fingers on the scarred wood of the table. "A few little girls were up late, doing each other's hair, when they spied a furtive-looking person darting along the road."

"And . . ." George prodded.

"Well, course, that led to all of them pressing their noses to the pane to see who it could be. Then they saw a woman placing the letter under a certain rock by your door." Sadie said the last with pursed lips, like she'd just swallowed a bitter lemon.

"A rock?" George asked inanely.

"The big gray one," Marshall said for no one's benefit but his own.

"Anyway, when this person started walking back . . . and the moonlight reflected off her face for a quick moment . . . the girls, bless their little spying hearts, saw clearly who the author of the notes was."

A knot formed in his stomach. "Well . . . ?"

Sadie looked at Marshall, then George, then Marshall again. "Boss, I hate to tell you this, but . . ."

He gripped the edge of the table. He was about to grab his best bargirl and pull the words out of her. "Come on Sadie . . . spit it out."

"Millicent Drovers," she whispered.

His hands went slack. "What?"

Sadie stood up in a hurry. "You heard me, Boss. I gotta go get Justine outfitted."

Horrified, Marshall looked at the letter.

George simply let out a low whistle. "Woo-whee."

Chapter Fourteen

Marshall sat stunned for a long moment, then took a quick swig of his whiskey. The liquor burned going down, which was a good thing, because for the moment, he was sure he was in the middle of a terrible dream.

Millicent Drovers, his secret admirer. He shook his head in dismay. Why hadn't she just gone and told him that she loved him? It would have been all right. He could have let her down gently, told her they just probably weren't suited.

Then, recalling their starry evening, and the previous evening at the opera, Marshall reevaluated things. Maybe they could have tried courting . . . seen how things felt between them. Or things could've just gone on. Normal, like. There wouldn't have been any picnics. Or betting pools.

He would have been spared the ribbing by the cowboys.

And the throng of angry fathers.

Minute by minute the anguish that he'd been put through came flooding back, full force. All of a sudden he was mad as a rooster who had never seen the light of day.

107

After slamming his glass back on the table, Marshall stood up and strode out of the bar, completely ignoring George and his questions, Justine in her new outfit, and Sadie with her speculative looks.

He had made a decision.

There was only one thing to do, and that was to go find Millicent herself and see what in the world was going on in that little head of hers. It just didn't stand to reason that she was being seen, gallivanting in her nightwear on the streets of Rocky River. Thing like that could give a girl a name for herself, she should know that.

Marshall felt assured and self-righteous as he sauntered down the street, tipping his hat to the ladies that he passed. He even used the time to prepared his speech to her.

First thing he'd do was question her about her whereabouts the previous evening. Ask her if she'd had any reason to traipse along the streets after midnight.

Then, after catching her red-handed in a lie, he would proceed for the kill. Stealthily he'd ask her about his letters. Try to catch her knowing about the second one when it was still practically a secret that he'd received more than one. Then, once she caught herself in his trap, he'd give her what-for about playing with people's emotions. Maybe even add a good dose of guilt, remind her that her pa would have been appalled at her behavior, not to mention what her mother would have said. God rest her soul.

Then, he'd reprimand her for inconveniencing him and half the town with his marriage plans. Just the thought of that picnic made him irritable again. How in the sam-hill was he going to explain his sudden desire for matrimonial bliss now?

He'd also force Millicent to recall the many number of

occasions that she'd had to correct his misconception about the letter in the first place, starting with that one meeting they'd had weeks ago, one her front steps.

Feeling both self-righteous and sanctimonious, Marshall strode up the front steps to Millicent's home and knocked smartly three times.

But no one answered.

Frowning, he pulled a watch out of his pocket. Ten A.M. Where could she be? At the mercantile? At a dress fitting somewhere?

He peered in a sparkling window, hoping for some sign of Millicent's whereabouts, then was brought up short by the voice of Millicent's neighbor, Mrs. Betty Sue Stover. She seemed a little agitated and fired up, to boot.

"Yes, ma'am?" he called out.

"I said, Mr. Bond, that Miss Millicent is not at home."

Leave it to Mrs. Stover to correct him loud enough for the whole street to know his business. Straightening up, he turned to find the lady perched at the other side of her open window, watching his every move. "Any idea where I might find Miss Millicent, Mrs. Stover? It's kind of important that I speak with her."

"No."

He tried again. "See, I'm needed down at the Dark Horse in an hour, and I wanted to get my business done quick-like."

Her eyes narrowed. "You've got sewing for her?"

"No ma'am. Our business is of a personal nature."

Mrs. Stover glowered. "Well, I'm sure I don't know what to think of that."

He gritted his teeth and tried another tack. "Mrs. Stover, which way did you see her go?"

She crossed her arms against the frame and looked to take his question very seriously. "Now, Mr. Bond, that'd be hard to say."

"Why's that?"

"Well, she left in a carriage," she said matter-of-factly, in just the way someone might mention that it had rained the night before.

"What?"

"Didn't look none too pleased about it, neither. I'm sure I heard her complain that she needed her hat, but Mr. Baxter didn't pay her no mind."

His heart skipped a beat. "Baxter?"

"I'm tellin' you, that Mr. Baxter just looked bound and determined to leave in a hurry. He told her in no uncertain terms that her straw bonnet would just be in the way where she was going," Mrs. Stover said conversationally, just like she was discussing the growth of her daises. " 'Course, Miss Millicent wasn't having any of that. There she went, sashaying back to the house, and pretty-as-you-please when she returned, one straw bonnet in her grasp."

"What did Edmund Baxter do while she was carrying on?"

"He just looked sullen, if you want to know the truth. Don't know what his mama would have thought of that . . . did you know he was a favorite of mine back when I was a schoolmarm?"

The whole idea struck him dumb . . . of Mrs. Stover being nice to small children, of Edmund ever being younger and halfway decent. "No, I did not," he said before he could remind himself that he had better things to do than to contemplate the childhood of Edmund Baxter.

"Oh, he was a curious fellow, he was," Mrs. Stover said,

a faraway look in her eyes. " 'Course, things changed when his ma died, and his dad took off and left him."

"How did he change?"

"Dropped out of school for one," Mrs. Stover recalled, almost as if it had been a personal affront. "Then he became a mighty hard worker, working for the Andersons until they began to pay him for his work in worthless pieces of land."

"Worthless?"

"It was thought to be that way at the time . . . 'course people have a different opinion about it, now that we all know it had a thick strain of gold in it."

"Did the Andersons try to get it back?"

"Of course they did, Marshall . . . but people in the town backed Edmund Baxter. What's fair was fair, after all," she said, nodding. "Then he went and repaid them by being a drunken fool."

They stood and pondered that fact for a moment before Marshall was once again drawn to the present. "So, you think she went with him against her will?"

"Don't rightly know," she answered, then seemed to ponder that thought as well. "My goodness, I hope he didn't force her to leave with him! He'd really have changed his stripes if he had . . . Why the nerve of some people!"

Marshall's heart felt as if it had been stomped on by a team of oxen. He felt the need to clarify, just in case he had misunderstood. "So you're saying that Millicent was abducted by Edmund Baxter? When was this? A few minutes ago? An hour?" At her vacant look, he practically yelled, "When did he leave with Millicent?"

She shook her head sadly. "That's one thing I just never understand about you young people. No manners in the world . . . raising your voice to an old lady, calling my neighbor by her given name, really."

"Mrs. Stover," he bit out, "how long ago did they leave?"

"Well, that'd be hard to say. I'd just fed Percy . . . you recall Percy, my prize-winning billy goat? Hmm . . . then I sat down and had a cup of coffee when I decided to look out the window to see what was happening at Miss Millicent's."

"Yes?"

"Not that I make it a habit to watch her house . . . just being neighborly, you know. It'd be what her pa would want, I believe."

Marshall fought the urge to pull the words out of her. "What time was that?"

"Oh. Hmm. Goodness, perhaps nine o'clock? Now Millicent did look lovely today, in a lavender-colored frock. Never did cotton to spendin' a fortune on clothes, but I do admire Millicent's work." She paused for breath, then continued, her words flowing, unabated. " 'Course, strange things have been going on at her house lately, with one thing and another . . ." she paused long enough to give him a frigid, knowing look.

"Did you happen to see which way they went in Mr. Baxter's buggy?"

She nodded. "Well, now that you mention it, I believe I surely did. They went right down toward the old mines. Now, that isn't much of a date, in my opinion. Personally I'd rather see Millicent continue her Saturday opera and dinner dates. She certainly looked lovely, and I had a good time spying to see who the next beau might be." Mrs. Stover patted her hair and then continued. "Like I said, I don't know what's gotten into her lately. Did you know she was traipsing around in her nightwear last night around one?"

"I heard about that, actually."

"Well, I could hardly believe my eyes when I peered at her, I tell you what."

He honestly couldn't take her prattling anymore. "You need to get more sleep, Mrs. Stover."

"I'll try, but I feel that I must warn you about my condition . . . I do believe it's catching . . ."

But Marshall didn't hear the rest of her words. He took off toward town to gather some help and his horse. Things had suddenly gone from bad to worse.

There was only one thing he felt certain about: Edmund was going to seriously regret his decision to ever even think about a future with Millicent Drovers.

Chapter Fifteen

"The thing of it is, Marshall," George said, once they were on the way to Baxter's mine, "is that even if we manage to get Millicent away from his clutches, we're not going to know what to do next."

Marshall knew exactly what he would do after they freed Millicent: string Edmund Baxter up by his toes. However, he aimed for a tone of detachment as they pointed their horses toward the west. "How do you figure that?"

"Come on, Marshall—what are *we* gonna do? Threaten him? Tie him up? Shoot him?"

All sounded like fine ideas. "Sheriff's on his way now, not twenty minutes out, I reckon," he answered simply. "He'll take care of things."

"You think?"

"I do," he said shortly, then gritted his teeth as he fought the urge to castigate his best friend. For heaven's sakes, he could sure use some positive thinking at the moment.

George looked ahead and nodded. "That's good. That's

good." He glanced at Marshall and chewed his lip, as if he was choosing his next few words carefully. "She's gonna be all right, you know. There's no telling why Baxter took off with her, but she'll be okay. Millicent's as tough a lady as any I've known. Shoot, she's probably already given him what-for for getting her dress dirty and is sitting on the edge of the camp, waiting for us to relieve her boredom!" He shrugged his shoulders. "I was just thinking that we needed a back-up plan, that's all."

"We'll have one," Marshall said steadily. "All we got to do is look out for Millicent. When we find her, her condition will tell us all we need to know. If Baxter's harmed one hair on her head, nobody's going to be asking why I beat him to a pulp. Heck, they'll be asking the opposite if I don't punch him out."

"That's a fact."

Marshall spent a good moment visualizing Edmund Baxter looking torn up and helpless, then continued. "Besides, I can't think that Baxter wants to hurt her anyway . . . he's just looking for some attention."

"I reckon so."

George's affirmations made him feel better already. "I bet you're right," he said with a little more enthusiasm. "Millicent has probably already given him a piece of her mind up one way and down the other."

Marshall chuckled at his words, then sobered as he recalled her tears the last time Baxter had threatened her. Shaking his head, he said, "Baxter sure has his due coming, though."

George nodded. "You'd think that scene in the saloon the other day would have been enough for him."

Recalling the threats of the men, Marshall let out a low

whistle. "You'd think so, but I guess he didn't take our words too seriously."

"I betcha those men who were with us have already saddled up and aren't far behind."

"Hope so."

They rode for a while longer, Marshall speaking softly to his horse when the mare stumbled on a rock.

The land around them looked green and lush for once. By June the bright green grass would fade to an olive shade and the ground would be dry and parched. The crisp air was invigorating, the scent of pine pungent and strong. It would have been a fine time to go for a ride, if the occasion wasn't so dire.

"I'm glad you came into town and got some help and didn't just ride out in a dither," George said after a few more minutes. "Lotta people are none too happy about these shenanigans. It's out of the ordinary for our Rocky River."

"It is."

"He's going to pay," he said again. "Marshall, you mark my words."

Marshall nodded, his eyes scanning the countryside for any signs of an earlier struggle. "Yes, he will," he said grimly. "I'll make sure of it."

They rode a little while longer. "There's a good thing about Miss Millicent, though," George said when the mine encampment finally came into view. "She's a level-headed woman. I imagine she's coping just fine, just like we thought."

"Let's hope so," Marshall said softly as he scanned the area. Baxter's carriage was visible, as was Millicent's favorite straw bonnet from its perch on the ground. Deep marks marred the ground. Every muscle in his body tensed again as he thought of the struggle that must have occurred.

Millicent just had to be all right, he told himself as he motioned to George to dismount over by the shade of one clump of pine trees. At the moment, he had to pray she would be. And he'd hope so, because otherwise he wouldn't be able to bear the thought.

Sitting atop a turned-over bucket in the suffocating dampness of the mine, it was all Millicent could do to breathe evenly. Nothing in her short life had ever prepared her for such a predicament! How could something so wrong just get worse and worse?

Not only had Edmund tricked her into thinking he needed her help, but he'd practically absconded her without a second thought.

Of course, looking back on things, Millicent knew she should have known the story that Edmund had told her didn't make a lick of sense. Of course Hannah Parson would never send Edmund to seek Millicent Drovers' assistance on anything. It just wasn't in Hannah's nature to be so vulnerable . . . or affable toward either Edmund or herself.

She should have known that from the start and cried out and sought Mrs. Stover's assistance.

But gosh, all she had thought about when Edmund came was that Hannah needed her exceptional sewing expertise to repair a torn dress, and that Edmund had changed his tune about marriage and wanted to just be friends.

She had been completely mistaken on both accounts.

Glancing at Edmund again, she watched his fingers steadily sort through rock and rubble. Recalled how he'd admitted to lying about Hannah's needlework needs . . . and then had boasted how he finally was taking charge of their relationship. After she realized they were going in the exact opposite direction of the town. Edmund was angry and troublesome and he disturbed her greatly. He'd raved about her prim disposition, her relationship with Marshall and her stylish clothes. And he hadn't been in any hurry to let her out of the buggy.

He was a peculiar man. He must be really out of sorts to resort to kidnapping her until she agreed to become his wife.

As if that type of coercion would ever work.

Of course, at the moment things weren't looking too good. The small cavern they were in smelled dank and foul, and there was barely enough room for the two of them. Shadows played along the walls and ceilings, making the rock walls feel like they were closing in. She could hear the faint scratching of a rat nearby. The situation could be described as uncomfortable at best.

She had no idea of how to escape, or even of how to defend herself against Edmund, should he suddenly turn ugly.

At least at the moment he seemed content to work next to her, guided by the dim candle that was perched on a tin plate to the left of him.

In direct contrast to her discomfort, Edmund Baxter looked almost at ease in their surroundings, as if his going to the dark floor of a mine in a three-piece suit was a common occurrence.

Millicent wondered if he'd done such a thing before.

Ever since they'd made their dreadful descent into the depths of the mine, he'd been ranting about his past. Just hearing about all the trouble he'd gotten into during his lifetime made her cringe.

Surely help had to be on the way.

She tried vainly to keep him talking. Eventually their conversation settled on the fateful day when he'd found his first strain of gold.

"That certainly must have been a grand day, Mr. Baxter."

He eyed her suspiciously. "It was. Biggest gold strike this town had ever seen."

"Thousands of dollars' worth."

His chest puffed up a bit with pride. "It was. I went right out and bought a new shirt as soon as I struck it rich."

Something about the way he spoke told Millicent that there was far more beneath Edmund's surface than mere madness. "A new shirt?"

He paused in his whittling. "Always had rags before then. Ma could never afford new clothes. We got them from the church. Used to have to turn my collars inside out to last longer." He said the last quietly, with some shame.

Millicent wondered if Edmund Baxter was merely just a lonely old man with no communication skills to speak of. The thought of him being more pitiful than frightening gave her strength to carry on. Hoping to keep him occupied, she asked, "After you bought that shirt, what did you purchase next?"

"A new pipe, then a pair of good boots," he said, then spoke in detail about each new item he'd purchased with his new riches.

She would have found the stories intriguing if she hadn't thought he looked slightly manic, or if she wasn't petrified by thoughts of what he was going to do to her. Into the bargain, things would have been far easier if she hadn't felt as if her chest had constricted so tightly, almost like her corset had been knotted up.

However, a talking Edmund was much preferred over a sullen, brooding one, so she became determined to keep him chatting—and at a safe three feet from her at all times. Unfortunately, the first goal was turning out to be much easier to achieve than her second. Like a checker on a board, he was managing to scoot his way toward her every few minutes. She was running out of space in their small confines.

Already she could smell his too-sweet cologne. She could only keep him at bay by encouraging him to talk about himself. When they finished the lengthy discussion about his clothing purchases, they moved onto the mechanics of mining.

Then various ways to pan for gold.

And finally the best ways to expand mine shafts. Millicent used her captivity as a learning opportunity, and asked a variety of questions. Edmund answered readily.

Currently, he was expounding on the merits of various forms of dynamite.

When he paused for breath yet again, she summoned up all of the conversational skills she'd fostered during her many Saturday night dates and thought of yet another question to ask. However, she was interested in his answer to this query. "Mr. Baxter, about your wealth . . ."

The question caught him off guard. He brushed back a strand of thick blond hair and looked at her warily. "Yes?"

"Have you ever thought about putting it to good use?"

He frowned. "I already give money to the women's and children's fund."

"That's very honorable, I'm sure . . . but I was thinking of using your money for a more, um . . . personal nature."

His eyes turned beady. "Like what?"

"Um, perhaps you ought to send for one of those mail-order brides that was mentioned in the *Denver Post*," she said quickly.

He looked wary. "Why?"

"Well, you could start anew. A girl from the East would be mightily impressed with your wealth and occupation. I'm sure she would be just dazzled by it."

His hands stilled. "You think?"

"Why, surely," she answered, even managing a small smile. "And just think, this Eastern girl might never have any idea about your somewhat humble beginnings."

He snorted. "Humble beginnings. That's one way of putting it."

A flicker of unease made her question his words. "I know you had a trying childhood. I did as well, with my mother dying so young."

"Girl, our childhoods were nothing alike. The charity baskets we got from the church twice a year were like gold to us. New clothes were scarce and almost unheard of. Some days the most food we'd ever get was from the trashcans in the back of some of the saloons."

She truly did feel for him. She hated the thought of anyone going hungry. "You've come so far," she said gently, forgetting for the moment that he was her kidnapper. "Sometimes it's good to just continue your progress, add polish to your, uh, shine."

"What are you saying?"

"Just that the past is a hard thing to overcome, is all . . ."

Her voice drifted off and she bit her bottom lip. Goodness, what was she speaking of?

Edmund scratched his head as he let the words sink in. "What do you mean?"

"That I know what I'm talking about, given my personal circumstances. I am an orphan myself, you know," she said primly, in just the way old Mrs. Hutchinson, the school-marm, had recited poetry.

Edmund thought for a moment then, as if he finally grasped her meaning and said, "My personal circumstances could change very quickly, if you would just accept my proposal. Marry me, Miss Millicent."

Millicent nibbled her lip again. There they were, back to that again.

After all, that was how this dreadful adventure had started. Edmund intended to keep her in the mine until she changed her mind about marrying him. Blackmail, pure and simple.

Of course, now that they were in this godforsaken hole in the ground, and had finally managed to have a real con-versation, Millicent was learning that there was more to Edmund Baxter than had previously met the eye. He was a man with a dark past and a murky future and a multitude of scars from living hard.

And he thought she was his key to a better life.

Yes, she was cold and damp and in serious danger of being touched by a rat. And she didn't appreciate being lied to or forced into places against her will. But she did have to admit that she wasn't particularly frightened, now that she realized Edmund was really just basically a lone-some bachelor.

Though she did wish to leave as soon as possible.

She had to think of something quickly. Surely Mrs. Stover had contacted Marshall or Sheriff Merry and they were on their way? "Um, well . . . there's an impediment to our future happiness together, something I've neglected to tell you beforehand."

He looked skeptical. "And that is?"

"I'm ah . . . already spoken for." She said the lie quickly, crossed her fingers behind her back, and tried not to analyze the rationale.

Edmund dropped the pick he had been holding. "You're what?"

She folded her hands in her lap and strived to sit a little straighter. "It's true. I'm already spoken for."

"To who?"

She gave him the most obvious choice. "Why, to Marshall Bond, of course. We've been secretly betrothed for quite some time now," she said as airily as she could. "We've um . . . been looking for the perfect time to announce it."

"Why have you been still going on your Saturday night dates?"

Good question. "Just to keep up appearances, of course."

"And the betting pool?"

"It was all merely harmless fun."

His eyes narrowed at her flip language. "Why didn't you tell me this earlier, before we got in the carriage?"

Why indeed? Truthfully, not a word she was speaking made a lick of sense. Thank goodness Edmund wasn't known for his intellect, merely a swelled head. She rolled a portion of fabric between her forefinger and thumb and thought fast. "Because we wanted to wait until Marshall's business was solvent. I promised him I wouldn't breathe a word of it until he allowed me to."

"Promised?"

She crossed her heart and hoped lightning wouldn't strike her down. "On my honor."

"And his business?"

"Yes?"

"How's it doing now?"

She truly had no idea. "Oh my, I believe that it's thriving! Oh what wonderful news." She forced herself to brighten. "Goodness, that means we'll be announcing our engagement at church this Sunday. I can't thank you enough for everything you've done! I hope you'll be there."

Edmund stared at her, as if trying to decipher her jumble of excuses. He looked beyond irritated, which, by the way, was exactly how she did not want him to be.

Millicent imagined he was trying to figure out how to either push her out of his mine as quickly as possible or how to wring her neck.

Silence stretched as they considered each other for a few long moments. Finally he spoke.

"I don't believe you."

Millicent had to sigh. Perhaps he was smarter than she had ever given him credit for. "I can prove that our engagement is real."

"How?"

"When Marshall comes to save me, I'll tell him that I broke our secret, and I'll allow him to announce it, right then and there."

Edmund snorted again. "When he comes to save you," he mumbled. Then he stared at her with his beady eyes one more time. "What about the letters?"

"I wrote them!" she exclaimed, relieved to finally be able to say something truthful.

"Seems pretty odd way of courting, to me."

"We didn't want to compromise my sterling reputation."

"Like you're doing now?"

"But *this*," she waved a hand around the confines of the room, "this abduction, is not my fault."

Edmund crossed his hands over his chest. "Seems to me that it isn't all my fault now, either. I'd never have lied or snatched you if I'd known you were engaged. Your lies, Miss Millicent Drovers, are what have gotten us to this crossroads." He said the last with a self-satisfied smirk, then pulled out a knife and a stray piece of wood and began to whittle.

What could she say to his statement? Unfortunately his words had merit. "Oh dear," she mumbled, then watched him chip away at the wood with trepidation.

Thank goodness they heard the shuffling of feet overhead. Otherwise, Millicent had no idea of what she would have done next.

Edmund's hands stilled. "What was that?"

Certain that it was Marshall or the sheriff, but not quite ready to trust her feelings, she said the first thing that came to mind. "Prairie dogs?"

A rustle, followed by the dim echo of voices, cascaded down the narrow shaft. Both of them looked up anxiously.

He frowned. "That don't sound like prairie dogs, woman. I would have thought that even you would know that."

"Well, I don't," she rattled. "After all, I've only seen prairie dogs from a distance. I've never attempted to room with one."

"Listen here," he snarled, but then was cut up short by a voice that could have only been Marshall Bond's.

"Baxter? You down there?"

Edmund grimaced as he stared at Millicent. "Now, where else would I be?"

Chapter Sixteen

Millicent wondered what Marshall thought of that statement, then didn't think of much at all as Marshall and George climbed down the ladder and then finally appeared, each looking madder than a wet skunk.

Millicent and Edmund shifted to make room for the two newcomers. The space was crowded and seemed more claustrophobic than ever.

Afraid to say anything to set Marshall's lips in a thinner line, Millicent held her position and waited.

But they did nothing.

If they were surprised that neither she nor Edmund jumped to their feet in greeting, neither Marshall nor George uttered a word. In fact, they just stood there, staring at Millicent sitting primly on a bucket, and at Edmund, who had returned to whittling on his stick.

Marshall's expression switched from worry to fury to complete confusion right before her eyes in the dim light. Millicent flexed her toes and tried to look calm.

George just looked at the two of them and said, "Well, you up to saving Miss Millicent now, Marshall?"

George's words seemed to make Marshall's lips thin even more. He glanced at her sternly, then finally said, "What's going on?"

Edmund glanced up at him, then down at his hands again as he sawed off a good chunk of wood from his stick. "Seems to me that I've stolen your intended by accident."

"Oh dear," groaned Millicent.

Marshall positively looked stunned. "You stole what . . . my *what*?"

Edmund stared hard at her. "Millicent here has been en-lightening me on the most recent developments in your love life."

"Such as?"

"First of all, I want to offer my congratulations on your thriving business."

"Oh dear," she muttered again.

Marshall's eyebrows rose so much, they just about left his face.

Edmund didn't seem to notice, he just kept talking. "Secondly—"

"Wait," Millicent called out, out of sheer desperation. Things were looking just dreadful. She was already in a deep hole . . . literally! This was no time to dig herself in even deeper. She practically threw herself at Marshall and was pleased when his arms opened to catch her.

"Umph," he groaned.

"It's all right, darling," she cooed and tried not to grimace at Marshall's narrowed eyes. "I told Edmund every-thing." She punctuated her last words with a sharp pinch to his upper arm, just in case he wasn't paying close attention.

He winced. "You have?"

Thank goodness he'd decided to play along. "Yes, dear. I told him how it's impossible that I marry him, because we've been secretly engaged for quite some time." She said the last words slowly, in case he was too stunned to absorb what she was saying, then held on tight when his arms went slack.

George stepped closer. In the dim light, Millicent noticed that he didn't look terribly pleased by the news. On the contrary, he pretty much looked put out. "You never told me about that."

Marshall scowled. "That's because—"

Millicent cut him off before he ruined everything. "We wanted to wait until your business was solvent. And guess what, it is! We can marry soon! Just as soon as we get out of this forsaken mine," she said cheerily as she attempted to scoot Marshall toward the ladder.

But no one seemed to have caught her hint.

Everyone just stayed put, each lost in his thoughts. Millicent glanced at the men, hoping for an ally, but not a one seemed forthcoming.

George looked offended and kept staring at Marshall with a wounded puppy look. Edmund went back to whittling his stick quietly. Chippings flew through the air with each downward stroke. And Marshall, well Marshall just kept trying to shove her off his person. Nobody seemed in any great hurry to leave their confines. Frustration built in her chest. Honestly, she was ready to have a hissy-fit right here in the mine, she was so bothered!

Things just weren't going as well as she had hoped.

Thank goodness she heard a group of voices above, their words muffled through the layers of rock. "Who's down there?" a voice that just had to be Sheriff Merry called out.

Edmund merely glanced at Marshall and thinned his lips. "Who's not here?" he grumbled.

Both Marshall and George seemed at a loss for words. Millicent supposed it was now up to her to save herself. "I am," she called up the shaft. "I'm here with Marshall, George, and Edmund Baxter."

"You doing okay?"

"We're all just peachy," George bit out.

"We're fine! Just a minute and we'll all climb on up." Eager to leave, Millicent scrambled out of Marshall's arms. He offered no opposition, just merely dropped his arms to his sides. "Marshall," she hissed. "Aren't you going to say anything?"

One eyebrow raised. "Why should I? I do believe you've said enough for all of us."

"Yeah," Edmund seconded.

"Why should you start talking now, anyway, Marshall?" George whined. "Heck, you never even thought to trust your best friend with your wedding plans." His blue eyes looked watery and flat. "Were you even going to invite me to the nuptials?"

Marshall stomped his foot. "For once and for all, I never . . ."

Millicent did some stomping of her own. One kid boot landed firmly on his shin.

"Yikes, Millicent," he cried. "What'd you go and do that for?"

"Millicent, Marshall? What's going on down there? Everything all right?" Sheriff said again.

"Everything's all right now," Millicent said, as brightly as she could, given the circumstances. "I, for one, am coming up right this second."

"What about Edmund? You need help roping him up?"

A prick of conscience touched her. "Oh, no, Edmund's fine. We just had a, ah, crossing of words."

"Crossing of words? What's that supposed to mean?" Sheriff Merry asked bitterly. "I'm missing lunch because of this . . . so are half the men here."

She looked at Marshall. "Help me."

He folded his arms over his chest. "No." Then, just to be ornery, he turned to Edmund. "You want her back? I could easily break our engagement."

Edmund glanced at Millicent, who was currently attempting to fix her hair before ascending the ladder. "You can take her. I'm thinking of trying out one of those mail-order brides that Millicent was telling me about, anyway."

That tidbit interested George. "I heard about those. What do you do, write to the girl for a while, then convince her to come out and marry you?"

Edmund shrugged. "Don't rightly know. I heard somewhere that you could get hitched by proxy, though. That might be the way to go. No backing out then." He said the last phrase with a hint of disdain. Millicent was sure it was directed at herself.

Appalled that Marshall was acting anything but smitten, along with the fact that she was more than ready to escape from the mine shaft, she let out a little sigh and began the climb up the ladder. "I'm going up," she said unnecessarily.

George stood up, also. "I'm right behind you, Milly."

Finally, when all four of them were standing in the sunlight, Edmund squinting uncomfortably, Sheriff Merry attempted to sort out their stories.

One by one, Sheriff Merry listened to them, his face becoming redder and redder with each new twist. Millicent thought he seemed especially perturbed when she tried to tell her part, but perhaps she only felt that way because Marshall just kept glaring at her, too.

Finally Sheriff Merry held up a hand and spoke. "Now, let me see if I've got this straight. As I understand it, Edmund Baxter lied to you, threatened you, kidnapped you, and tossed you in the bottom of the mine, but now you hold no hard feelings toward him?"

Millicent shifted uneasily but stood firm. "Correct."

Anton McKenna chimed in from his perch on a russet mare. "And you two have secretly been betrothed for months and never told anyone?"

Marshall opened his mouth to reply, but George beat him to it. "They didn't tell a soul," he said forlornly. "What do you think of that?"

"I don't rightly know," Anton said slowly, anger building in his expression. "Did Chrissie know about this, Millicent?"

"No, she didn't."

"Marshall, you never told anyone?"

He just glared. "Absolutely not."

"But you believe Miss Millicent's story, Baxter?"

Edmund nodded. "Sure I do. Why wouldn't I? After much consideration, I don't believe that Miss Millicent's the girl for me, anyway. I'm going to try my hand at one of those mail-order brides."

Several men responded to his statement with comments and a few scattered questions. Millicent tried to look proud that she was now free from her confines and not merely a cast-off of Edmund's.

Only Marshall stood quietly.

Sheriff Merry stared hard at him. "Don't see that your actions have been very chivalrous, Bond. You've been playing fast with a multitude of impressionable girls' emotions, as well as seriously compromising Miss Millicent's pristine reputation. What do you have to say for yourself?"

At first it looked as if he had nothing to say at all. Marshall just stood silently, his expression as closed as a storm shutter. Then finally he spoke. "I . . . don't have anything to say, Sheriff. I believe it would be best if Millicent and I spoke about this later in private."

Millicent bit her lip. Of course Marshall wasn't going to say a word against her in front of everybody . . . he wasn't the kind of man to publicly humiliate a girl. But to realize that she had brought all of this misfortune on herself and Marshall was hard to take. She owed him so much.

No one seemed quite certain how to take his pigheadedness. Sheriff Merry glanced at the men and at George, one eyebrow raised in confusion. The six other men just stood their ground, angry self-righteousness in their bearing.

Feeling more and more guilty for all the trouble that she had caused, Millicent stumbled for something to say to fill the void. "My goodness, it sure would be nice to go home now," she said inanely.

Marshall just looked at her with disdain, let another minute pass, then finally spoke.

"I can only apologize for any grievances that this mixup has caused," he said stiffly. "I can only say that I was

sworn to secrecy by Millicent and that my word is something that I, as a gentleman, feel honor bound to keep."

"Oh, Marshall," Millicent said as she stepped forward
and then clung to his arm. She even attempted to hold tight
as his muscles tightened and he tried to loosen herself from
his grip.

However, if the other men in the vicinity noticed Marshall's complete lack of enthusiasm regarding his intended's charms, they said nothing. Most just nodded their
heads, gave Marshall a look of loathing, and then spoke to
the sheriff about taking Baxter into custody.

Millicent knew without a doubt that before long all the
men would have told their wives about today's escapade
and that both she and Marshall would have to do a lot of
work to earn the townspeople's trust again.

Within a few minutes, everyone had begun their trek
home, Millicent riding in Edmund Baxter's buggy with
George. Their mood was far from happy, and it was evident
that each held malevolent feelings toward the other.

Millicent had never been so happy to reach her own little
clapboard home. Already she planned to take a long bath
and change her dress. The dank smell of the mine seemed
to have permeated her clothes and body.

But her plans weren't meant to be. "Millicent, we need
to talk," Marshall said as soon as George left them to go
visit with Chrissie.

"We'll do that, real soon."

An eye twitched. "I think not. Matter of fact, I think it'd
be a mighty good idea if we just say our piece right now,
get things out in the open."

Oh dear. "Right now?" she hedged. "I was just thinking

how glorious a bath would feel, after my abduction and all."

"You'll survive a little while longer."

She really was not ready for this conversation! "But . . ."

"Frankly, I'm afraid what will happen if we even postpone this discussion even for five minutes," he said, cutting her off. "I'm afraid if I don't say once and for all what's on my mind, I may just forget that I'm a gentleman and give you the thrashing that you surely deserve!"

She was positively shocked. "Marshall!"

"Don't you 'Marshall' me. It's time to speak frankly, don't you agree?"

"Oh yes. Completely," Millicent responded, though truthfully she felt as if she had just agreed to a far worse punishment. With great trepidation she sat down on her porch swing.

Chapter Seventeen

Reluctantly Millicent glanced at Marshall. He sat on the planks of her front stoop, his left hand bearing most of his weight, his legs stretched out on the steps below. Usually in such a position he would give the illusion of someone who was carefree, relaxed, but at the moment it looked as if he was about to explode. Maybe it was because his body looked rigid and his right hand held a cigar in a death grip.

Or maybe it was the aggravated glare that he wore like a mask . . . directed her way.

A shudder passed through her. Tears teased her eyes, she blinked them away. Finally, finally, she felt the strong sense of misgiving and guilt that she had known she should have been feeling from the get-go, when all this started.

As she fidgeted with her dress, Millicent tried to think of something, anything to diffuse his temper. However, nothing seemed to be forthcoming at the moment. Of course, that shouldn't have come as a great surprise.

After all, what could she say? Somehow things had gotten out of control, and she, not Marshall, had held the power to get things back to normal. But instead, she'd spurred things on, and it had all backfired. Not only had she played false with Marshall's emotions, she'd drawn in a whole cast of characters from town into her charade.

She glanced at him again. He was puffing on his cigar and staring out at the field across from her home. She glanced in the same direction, and remembered another evening, not too long ago, where they had looked at the stars over that field and shared a wonderful, magical kiss. She left the porch swing, seated herself next to him, and cleared her throat, ready to say anything to put things to rights.

However, Marshall was the one to break their silence. "Millicent," he said, finally turning to look at her frankly, "we need to talk."

"Yes." It was hard to meet his gaze. She concentrated on the grooves running through the planks of wood.

"Things need to change . . . I believe."

Waiting for him to get to the point was pure torture, but Millicent held her tongue. "Yes," she said again, this time punctuating her word with a slight nod.

For some reason, the head nod seemed to spur him on. Marshall sighed deeply, then spoke again, his voice sounding scratchy, as though he was pulling each word out. "Millicent, the way I see it, things have just been going from bad to worse in my life."

Her head popped right back up. Even though she felt completely contrite, she wasn't about to let him blame all the troubles in his life on her! "Now, Marshall."

His eyes narrowed. "Don't you 'Now Marshall' me. You

ought to feel some kind of remorse. After all, you started this whole thing."

"I know that."

"So . . . ?"

"I feel that I should point out that it wasn't my fault the wind blew my note to Chrissie to your front door."

"Are you honestly going to spar with me over who had been at fault these last few weeks?" he asked, each word incredulous.

She didn't care for his tone, or the rather alarming look in his eyes. "Perhaps we shouldn't continue this conversation until you are in more control of yourself."

A hand whipped out and grabbed her by the shoulder when she attempted to stand up. Though she could have easily pushed away his hand, she remained where she was. "You are not going to go anywhere. You are going to sit right here next to me and let me say my piece."

"Please remove your hand from my person," she retorted, although in truth his grip was not as worrisome as it was disconcerting . . . on the contrary, his palm sent yet another wave of warmth through her, just like his touch always did.

"Please do me the honor of listening to me."

His words, such a parody of his usual good manners, unnerved her. She'd never seen Marshall so infuriated in her whole life. But seeing that he was waiting for an appropriate answer, she nodded her head in a most distinct show of grace and said, "You may continue." After all, that was the very least she could do, right?

Her demeanor must have unnerved him, too, because when he spoke again, his words were quiet, steadier. He glanced at her for a moment before removing his hand, then raked those fingers through his hair. "All right, what do you suppose we should do now? We've got a fake engagement to consider. My guess is that this news is going to spread like wildfire before we know it. Not only that, a lot of people are going to think we deceived them intentionally, and they won't think too highly of that, either. We should have a plan about what to do."

Everything he was saying made sense. "All right."

"I mean, think about all those men you've been seeing . . . what are they going to say when they find out that you've been letting them take you out but have been planning nuptials with me on the sly?"

She chewed on her lip. "But actually . . ."

"Millicent, that's how people are going to see it."

He was right . . . exactly right. Oh, how could things have gotten so messed up? "I know you're right."

He nodded. "Good." Marshall stood up, turned to the window and glanced outside. He took another puff on his cigar. Long minutes passed. An owl hooted in the distance. Millicent wrapped a shawl more tightly around her shoulders. And waited. Marshall looked as if he was having an argument with himself and that no one was winning. His hand tightened on the porch railing and then fell to his side. Finally he turned back to her.

"In addition," he said quietly, "I suppose we ought to figure out what we desire to happen to us."

His words left her confused and wary. She glanced at his face to attempt to see what he was thinking, but his expression was shuttered. "Happen to us?"

He glanced at her sideways. "Tell me honestly—have you ever imagined that we'd be married one day?"

"Goodness, no," she blurted, then immediately felt that familiar blush climb her throat. That wasn't quite the truth.

Suddenly, she had no desire to continue the web of lies that she'd been spinning for him. "Marshall, actually . . . there was a time when I had dreams of us together."

He stepped toward her, the expression in his eyes interested and alert. "Is that right?"

"Yes, as a matter of fact . . . at one time, why, I must admit that I had quite a fascination toward you . . . at um, one time." Pressing her hand to her chest, Millicent heaved a sigh of relief. She had done it; she'd finally admitted the truth about her feelings for him. It hadn't been so bad, after all.

"At one time?"

"Yes," she answered, feeling as if things weren't going well at all. Oh, what was happening? She'd never imagined actually telling Marshall of her interest! Oh, what he must think of her right now? She sneaked a glance at him from under her eyelashes.

He smiled slowly. A wicked gleam appeared in his eyes.

"Marshall," she uttered, waiting for a reply.

"Now, this puts a whole new spin on things, doesn't it?"

She couldn't figure out if he was teasing or not. "What do you mean?"

"I've imagined that, also."

She blinked. "You have?"

His gaze was warm and lingering. "Once or twice."

"Oh." Once again she was drawn to him, not just to his tenderness, but now to an underlying facet of their relationship . . . something not quite tangible but did feel in her reach. She glanced at him again, took in his chambray homespun shirt, his brown pants, the scuffed boots. He looked so familiar—yet new. She fought the urge to touch him, to see if he felt different next to her . . . if she would react differently to his touch.

"What if . . . just for the sake of it . . . what if we envisioned ourselves married? What do you think it'd be like?"

Millicent shivered as his words shimmied down her spine. His voice was gentler than she'd heard it in a long time. As gentle as the day he held her at her pa's funeral and assured her that she would never be completely alone. She glanced at him through her dark lashes. He was now leaning against the porch railing. His body looked relaxed, but his expression was severe.

She swallowed. "Well, I always pictured us happy," she said lamely.

"Is that all?"

"Well, no. I, um, supposed that we'd be comfortable together."

He nodded. "I've thought that, too."

They shared a small smile, then sat in silence for a while. Finally Marshall spoke again.

"I suppose that you'd expect me to give up the Dark Horse if we were married. Have a more respectable occupation."

"Goodness, no."

He stared at her, surprised. "It wouldn't bother you, being a saloonkeeper's wife?"

"Of course not, Marshall. Why, you think of the strangest things."

A crease formed between his brows. "You don't understand . . . there are many women, ladies in town, who wouldn't care to associate with you after that . . . even with your esteemed reputation and all." He spoke the words slowly, as if he was afraid that she wouldn't catch his meaning otherwise. She sought to reassure him.

"That wouldn't bother me in the slightest," she whispered, as she approached him, stopping a mere foot away.

He looked doubtful. "You say that now, but one day, when someone doesn't invite you to tea, or Mrs. Anderson suddenly decides she doesn't need any more gowns, why I'm sure it would."

Her heart went out to him; it was so rare to see even a flicker of doubt in his disposition. "I believe you're wrong, Marshall," she said gently, laying a hand on his arm in reassurance. The muscles contracted at her touch. "See, I wouldn't be a saloonkeeper's wife. I would be Marshall Bond's wife," she corrected. "There's a difference."

"They're one and the same, honey."

"No, they're not. One is a man, the other is merely an occupation," she retorted.

Marshall chuckled at her prim tone. "I'd be out late; you'd rarely have me home at night, except for Sundays, of course."

"On the other hand, I'd have you with me during the day," she answered, not quite able to keep a dreamy tone from her voice. "We'd get used to it, I imagine."

His left palm covered her hand on his arm, his thumb lazily tracing her knuckles. Once again she thought of how different his body was from hers . . . his thumb so calloused where hers was smooth, the muscles in his arm so defined where hers was soft.

"Where have you envisioned us living?" he asked.

"I suppose over the saloon or at my home."

He nodded. "I guess we could make things work out."

His words were puzzling. She decided to turn the tables.

"Marshall, what about you? Have you ever thought seriously about the two of us together, or just a time or two?"

He chuckled and laid his cigar in a metal dish on the ground. "Actually, I have thought about it."

"And?"

"And I imagined some of those things, also."

"But other things, too?"

He swallowed hard. "Yes."

"Such as?"

His gaze flickered over her figure. "Well, Mill, my thoughts were of . . . a more personal nature."

His gaze was so different than his usual friendly look that it caught her off guard for a second. She felt attractive and pretty, in a way that had nothing to do with the style of her gown. For once she felt as if her allure to him was simply because he saw her as a woman.

Attractive. Desirable.

She struggled to keep up the conversation. "As in children?"

He coughed. "Excuse me?"

"I just wondered if your thoughts had ever concentrated more on our home life, you know . . . children, dinners, quiet time when it would be just the two of us."

"Actually, my feelings have turned in that direction before."

Feeling encouraged, she squeezed his arm in reassurance. "Tell me, then."

He actually reddened in the bright moonlight. Millicent watched, fascinated, as a flush of color flowed across his neck. "I don't feel that my thoughts are all that significant, other than sharing with you that I have, indeed, thought of our children and our time together."

They sat in silence again, Marshall glancing at his feet. He slid her hand down his arm to clasp his own. "I guess we now know where we stand with each other, at least dream-wise."

"That we do."

"Time's a-wasting. We better come up with a plan."

Already envisioning the carrying out of another plan made her cringe. There was no way that she wanted to be in charge of any nefarious plot again! "I've already planned too much. Why don't you decide something and I'll go along with you?"

"All right, if you insist." He waited a few seconds, then turned fully to her. "As a matter of fact, I believe that I've come up with something that should suit our purposes nicely."

She could hardly wait to hear it. "And it is?"

"I think, Millicent, that we should plan to really get married," he stated in a firm tone that left no room for argument.

She could only stare at him in shock.

Chapter Eighteen

"Married?"

"Well, don't sound so surprised," Marshall chided. "It was your idea in the first place."

"But I didn't mean it. I was trying to get away from Edmund Baxter!"

"Edmund has already insisted that he would have never abducted you if he had thought you were already engaged."

"But . . . but . . ."

"Calm down, Millicent," Marshall said calmly. "We don't have to rush into things. We could do things slowly."

"How slow?"

"We could take our time, if that's what you wanted. Maybe have another date . . . or two."

"A date or two? We've hardly even had one!"

Marshall just ignored her and kept talking. "Although, for appearances, I think we ought to seriously consider the possibility of a marriage in the near future."

Marshall was planning things so fast that she could hardly keep up. "Say again?"

"With everything that's been going on . . . I think matrimony is a little inevitable . . . in my opinion, so we might as well get it over with."

Her mind was spinning. "Inevitable?" Lord, she sounded like a parrot.

"You know that having an actual wedding might be the only thing to get us back into the proper social standing. And we could say that we've already gone out together several times, formally."

"Such as?"

"Well, the other night at the opera. And the evening of the picnic . . . and tonight, of course."

"Tonight?"

He smiled. "It shouldn't be too hard to classify this evening as a date . . . everyone knows that after I rescued you I came here, to your house. Tonight should count."

"How can you say that?" she asked, incredulous. "I've been abducted, reprimanded, and embarrassed in front of a band of men this evening . . . not to mention all of the things that have been going on between the two of us."

He smiled wickedly. "All the more reason to say we've been courting. Don't worry, things will work out soon."

"Courting! This—" She motioned to her porch in disgust, "is not courting . . . this is a . . . ah . . . a planning meeting."

He seemed amused by her semantics. "Your neighbor, Mrs. Stover, would probably beg to differ."

Millicent removed her hand from his clasp and folded it firmly across her chest. "Mrs. Stover has way too much to say about my life as it is."

"Everything that she had to say wasn't all bad, you know."

"Believe me, I've heard plenty."

"In any case, I'm sure that Mrs. Stover would call me sitting here with you in the moonlight . . . sparking."

"Sparking?" she scoffed. "I'll have you know that a couple is only sparking if they are kissing, which, most assuredly, we are not."

Marshall walked right up to her, pulled her toward him, and kissed her hard. He pressed his lips to hers and held off any further protestations, not that she actually had any to make. From the moment they'd made contact she melted. In fact, all she cared to do once his sweet lips met hers was to snake her hands up around his neck and hold on tightly, because the world outside his embrace all of a sudden seemed strange and unfamiliar.

Without a doubt, she knew that this was the place that she needed to be . . . in Marshall's arms, against his chest, tasting his lips, reveling in his kisses.

She could still smell the faint aroma of his bay rum aftershave . . . the lingering scent of his cigar . . . and felt his rough cheeks against her soft ones . . . and hoped that he would never leave.

But he did.

He lifted his head just inches from hers. "I'll see you tomorrow?"

His voice was rough. She merely stared dumbly at him, all too aware that he had left her body aching for more Marshall Bond. "Uh huh."

"And we both agree that marriage is in our best interests . . . at least sometime in the future?"

Was this her long-awaited marriage proposal?

"Marshall, now wait a min—" It was so hard to concentrate; her body seemed only to want to be focused on the feel of his arms, the taste of his lips.

"You know I care for you, Millicent."

"I . . . care, too."

"That's good." The corners of his lips twitched as he gazed at her, then he leaned down to taste her again.

Millicent closed her eyes for a brief moment. A hot, unfamiliar feeling pooled in her stomach. Unconsciously she reached for him again. She raked her fingers through his hair, and captured his body against hers, all too eager to reclaim the feeling that she'd had in his arms just a moment earlier.

But all too soon he stepped back. Cool air wafted between them. Goosebumps rose on her arms.

"I'll have come up with something to get everyone in town behind us by then," he promised.

"All right."

"Don't worry, darlin'. Everything will be all right."

Millicent just nodded. Her lips felt swollen, her mouth too thick to speak.

He took another step away from her. "You'll be able to sleep tonight? You don't have too many lasting effects from today's adventures?"

She stared at him dumbly, only able to think about the feel of his arms about her. "No, I'll be all right."

He nodded. "Good." He slipped his hat on, and stepped down the stairs before turning back to gaze at her just one more time. "Get on to bed, now, honey," he said in that oh-so-gentle tone that he seemed to only use when he felt the most tenderest of emotions. "You don't want to catch cold now."

"All right," she said yet again, in that same oh-so-comforting daze. "I'll go on in."

He grinned quickly at her words, and she caught a sudden flash of teeth. "Good night, Millicent. See you in the morning."

And just when Millicent remembered how to raise her hand to wave good bye, she realized that he had already left.

Unconsciously she sniffed the air, looking for any sign that Marshall still lingered. But she could only smell the wood burning in Mrs. Stover's kitchen.

And with that, she wandered inside and off to bed, not even caring that she had yet to take her bath.

Chapter Nineteen

The rest of his plan wasn't much, Marshall admitted to himself, if, truth to tell, he even dared to analyze it that thoroughly.

After all, how was he going to able to persuade the majority of the population in Rocky River to put aside their prejudices against him and give him another chance? How were girls like Hannah Parson going to forget about marriage bets and picnics and unspoken promises and welcome his own nuptials in their place? Marshall sighed wearily as he climbed out of bed and poured water from a pitcher and washed his face.

However, he did know, without a doubt, that something had to be done or he would never find himself or Millicent in good standing in Rocky River.

He'd gone to bed the previous night thinking only about Millicent . . . in ways he'd previously been reluctant to ever ponder.

But he hadn't been able to help it. Last night was as

close to her as he'd ever been, both physically and emo-
tionally. For once, their boundaries had been redefined and
he'd found himself stepping gingerly into uncharted terri-
tories . . . and been welcomed with open arms. Now he
couldn't wait to return there, to kiss her again, to feel her
slim body curved into his . . . to one day take all the pins
out of her hair and do any number of things that only good
company would call husbandly.

He wanted to love her.

He wanted to call her his wife.

But, more importantly, he wanted Millicent to be proud
to be in that position. And that's where all of the planning
began. As he remembered the look of scorn that George,
Anton McKenna, Sheriff Merry and the others had directed
his way, he knew that he needed to make tracks fast.

Something had to happen to make everyone overcome
their hard feelings and begin to see he and Millicent as a
couple, he realized as he shrugged on a worn linen shirt
and slicked back his hair with his fingers. Over and over
again he reviewed the many episodes that had clouded his
life in the past two weeks. Mentally he recalled various
conversations he'd had with others . . . trying to think of
something to put into place so he and Millicent could start
anew. And that's when the thought struck—right in the
middle of putting on his boots.

Spring fever.

Sadie had said the whole town was infected with it. People were looking for love. They wanted to find it, too. All
that was lacking in Rocky River was an opportunity to
catch it. There needed to be an occasion for each person to
procure their own bit of love sickness.

And that's when it came to him. Another picnic.

Marshall felt sure it was a way to get everyone together and moving on past the rumors and gossipmongers that seemed to have settled into their town. Simply, having a grand picnic sounded like a good idea.

Of course, he'd had to make sure that there would be people there to join him and Millicent. That was where he'd need to do some serious groveling. People were going to need to be persuaded to come to the picnic, and he needed them to help him put his plan into action.

Oh, surely, he'd make certain that Millicent did her part . . . but to his way of thinking, he had no choice. There was his future to think about . . . and it was going to go nowhere fast unless he and Millicent were in wedded bliss.

He left the house feeling better about things than he had in the last week. And when he walked down the street and tipped his head to Mrs. Thomas, he merely grinned when she obstinately looked the other way. After all, what could he do, besides enlist his friends' help and hope for the best?

'Course, the enlistment part wasn't going to be all that easy, Marshall realized once again as he settled himself across from George and his friend began to reprimand him for his ways rather publicly.

He steeled himself, tried to hold his temper while George went on and on about trust, truth, and recollections of a certain fishing trip when they were ten.

"Now George," Marshall chided, shaken that he'd had the nerve to bring up something that both had agreed, by pinky promise, no less, that would be forgotten.

"I'm telling you, Marshall. Those are the things that are the very basis of our friendship."

"Just because we ate those trout when we said we tossed them back . . ."

George held up a hand. "There you go again, breaking another vow."

"Confound it! What do you want me to say? I'm sorry? I did already."

George just stared at him, as solemn as an Indian Chief.

"Come on. You know everything that happened in the last couple of days hasn't been my fault."

"A good part of it was."

Marshall pulled out a cheroot from his pocket. "I tell you . . . if you knew the whole story you'd be thinking differently."

George slammed a hand on the table. Several other diners looked up curiously, some not even pretending to do anything but eavesdrop. "What do you mean the whole story?"

"Will you hold it down? I don't need everyone in here to know my business."

"Why? It'd just be lies, anyway," he grumbled. "I don't know what you'd have to say that would even be close to reality!"

Marshall took a long draw from his cigar then finally gave into the inevitable. "All right. You want the truth? Well, here it is, and take hold of it in all its glory: I lied."

George just looked disgusted. "That's what we've been talking about."

"No, I lied *yesterday*."

"To who?"

"To everyone," Marshall admitted wearily. "Millicent and I've never been secretly engaged. Heck . . . you know that for a while there I'd been trying to get her married to someone myself. But she made that up because she was scared of Edmund pressuring her in that hole in the ground, and then Edmund told us, then everyone else . . . what else could I have done?"

George just stared at him like an elk during mating season . . . interested but unready to trust. Then finally his eyes narrowed and he looked every inch the formidable fighter he'd been in his youth. "So what are you going to do now?"

Marshall fingered his cigar, rubbed his thumb along the rough seam of it. "Millicent and I did some talking last night. We've come to believe that matrimony would be in the best interest of our future."

George's hand clenched. "Has your head taken leave of your body? Millicent Drovers has trapped you, no doubt about it."

"She hasn't exactly. And once more . . . I've realized that I have strong feelings for Millicent."

"What do you mean?"

Still eyeing George's ready fist, and recalling a time when George's temper had gotten the best of him during their teenage years at a barn dance . . . Marshall began some fast talking.

He talked about the mistaken note, and Millicent's reluctance to tell him the truth. He described his evenings with her, and his feelings that had been anything but brotherly. Actually, he'd had to sit with George for quite a while and fully tell him the depth of Millicent's scheme before George had unbent enough to both relax his hand and offer his help. Then, when Marshall had finally clarified that Millicent's plans, though misguided, had held no true bad intentions, George warmed up sufficiently enough to accompany him when they went to go find Millicent and make some firm plans.

Of course, Marshall didn't even think of sharing with

George a particular idea that had begun to form in his mind. Lord, he knew what George would say about that! But a certain plan had begun to take form in his head, a certain idea that brought him great pleasure. It was about something that could take place at that picnic that would bring both he and Millicent eternal bliss.

As he weighed the possibilities, Marshall made a mental note to check in with the preacher to see if he was available on Sunday.

For her part, Millicent had much of the same kind of conversation with Chrissie, a chat full of apologies and honest feelings. It was followed by a firm promise to never again lie to her best friend in such a fashion. Then, once Chrissie was finally happy with her, they accompanied George and Marshall to Lindy's, their favorite restaurant. Once there, Marshall shared his idea about a town picnic with the rest of them. After a few questions, everyone was ready to formulate the logistics of their spring fever plan.

"I'm thinking it just might work, Marshall," Chrissie said, sounding pleased. "All the girls in town were looking forward to your Sunday picnic, even when they thought they weren't invited."

Marshall sipped on his coffee. "Not to sound full of myself or anything . . . but you don't think they were just looking for matrimony?"

Chrissie's eyes lit up. "That was part of it . . . but I think it's safe to say that Marshall Bond wasn't the only attraction." She smiled broadly then. "People like getting dressed up and eating lunch outdoors. They like having something different to do. This picnic event will give them just that."

"If we give them an invitation, people will come, if only

to see who else made the effort." George nodded. "The only problem I can see is that we're goin' to have to make a whole slew of invitations and deliver them, too."

"It needs to be secret-like, or it will spoil the surprise," Chrissie added. "We need to just invite people to go to the park at a set time, but not give too many details."

Millicent tilted her head. "I don't know how much a surprise we can hope for, truthfully. After all, everyone is going to see the direct correlation between the invitations to picnic and Marshall's original one."

"Yes, but that won't matter, if we put the right kind of spin on things," George pointed out.

"Such as?"

"We'll need to make it special."

"Yes, it needs to be the social event of the season . . . people will want to attend, and be a part of it," Millicent said, catching on. "Hmm. I wonder if we could seek the musicians and singers from the opera house to our cause?"

"Don't see why not," Marshall replied. "A party's a party, for most concerned, anyway."

"Then it's settled," George declared. "We'll need to write some invitations, pass them out . . . and be prepared to do some positive Marshall propaganda."

Marshall scowled. "Thanks."

"No problem." George grinned. "I'll be in charge of that part myself."

Millicent chuckled as she watched the interplay between Marshall and George. Once more things seemed to be back on track between them. "I think we should go visit Sadie, too. She knows everyone and is one of the most organized people I've ever met. I bet she'll have some great ideas about where to proceed from here."

Marshall glanced at her quickly. "Are you sure about that, Milly? I really do admire Sadie, but she is just an employee at the Dark Horse to some people." He looked wretched as he tried to convey his feelings without offending Millicent or ruining Sadie's good name. "I mean, some ladies don't care to associate with—"

"I think today would be a perfect time to strengthen my acquaintance, Marshall," said Millicent pertly. "Who knows, Sadie and I may come to rely on each other for quite a bit in the future."

"I know that, darlin', but you might want to consider . . ."

"How perfect she's going to be for our plan," Millicent finished with a smile. "Don't worry, dear. It will be all right."

"Darlin'? Dear?" Chrissie clanked her spoon down. "Pardon me, but what else is going on between the two of you that you've neglected to tell us about?"

Millicent couldn't think to do anything but chew on her lip and stare at Marshall. After all, how could she articulate the wealth of emotions that she felt for him? That she was fascinated by him? Treasured his friendship? Loved Marshall Bond?

But her embarrassment didn't seem to make a bit of difference to George. He just eyed the couple across from him for a good long minute before replying. "There's just no telling, Chrissie. I still can't keep up with their ornery mood swings. Heck, it's like Marshall and Millicent are on their own mixed-up carousel . . . going round and round on their own course," he said glumly. "But don't worry, if we stand here long enough, when they come round again something else in their relationship will be different. I'm learning that real fast."

Chrissie laughed. "That sounds like a fitting description for Rocky River's most mixed-up couple."

Chapter Twenty

A few hours later, they all met with Sadie to enlist her help. Sadie's aid was critical, due to the fact that she had a reputation for saying whatever was on her mind, and also for the fact that she had no patience for fools. That was part of her charm . . . well that, and the fact that many thought that she had a gift for telling stories and was lovely, to boot.

"So we're all going to become letter writers?" she asked, one auburn-tinted eyebrow arched.

Marshall nodded.

"And you want me to help deliver them, too?"

"If you're willing."

Sadie looked at Marshall for a few minutes. Millicent was hardly able to breathe, she was so worried about how Sadie might react. Finally Sadie looked ready to speak.

"Boss, I've worked for you for a long time," she began slowly, "even back when we only sold that Monongahela."

"Monongahela?" Millicent asked.

"Don't worry about that," Marshall murmured. "It's a type of whiskey." Then louder, he said, "I know how hard you've worked, and I've always appreciated it, too."

"We've been through a lot of things together . . . from hiring on help, to building this saloon, to the time when I found myself in a family way. . . ."

"I know that, Sadie."

"All that said, I think I should tell you that if I do this too . . . this letter writing, delivering campaign . . . I'm gonna need a raise."

Marshall's answer was instantaneous. "You got it."

"I've got a two-year-old to feed, now."

"He's a good 'un, that's a fact. You've got your raise, Sadie. We'll talk about the details tomorrow morning."

Sadie sighed heavily, as if the whole conversation had worn her out, though Millicent did notice a spark of amusement in her eyes. "All right then," Sadie pronounced. "Hand me some paper and I'll set to work."

After a few more discussions, they were ready to put their plan to action. Sadie roped Justine into helping and then everyone got organized. After all, both Marshall and Millicent agreed that they needed to do whatever was necessary to win Marshall back into the good graces of Rocky River's patriarchal community. There was a whole mess of fathers with a bone to pick with him, and business had been kind of slow, to boot.

After noticing Marshall's and George's terrible penmanship, Millicent, Chrissie, Justine, and Sadie decided to tackle the hundred invitations themselves, each taking twenty-five. Marshall gallantly offered to keep Millicent company at a corner table in the saloon, a good two hours before the Dark Horse was set to open for the evening's business. Within minutes, Millicent had a pile of paper, a newly sharpened quill, and Marshall by her side.

Sadie wanted to get a few things done first, so she, Ernestine, and Frank stayed at the front of the bar and proceeded to polish the woodwork and organize the glasses.

As she observed them, Millicent had a first taste of what actually being a part of the inner workings of the saloon entailed. Marshall's attention centered upon a stack of communication to sort through, as well as updates from Sadie and Frank about the stock of liquor and food. He read through them cursorily, giving her an impression that these were tasks that he had done a hundred times. Once again she took the time to daydream about what their future might entail. Pretty soon she would know all these people—have lunch with them—and maybe even understand exactly what kind of a whiskey Monongahela was.

"Marshall?"

"Yep?"

"You know how we talked about getting married one day?"

A secret smile played on his lips. "I do."

"Well, one day, when that happens . . . if that happens . . . I think should stay here during the week and at my house on the weekends," she said, stretching her fingers after writing invitation number eleven.

Marshall didn't look convinced. "Honey, that's probably not such a good idea. The Dark Horse is far from anything even resembling a ladies' social club. The men can get rowdy, especially during a round-up or when someone strikes a good streak of gold. You might be happier being at your home most nights."

"But then how would I see you? I thought sometimes you stayed busy until the early hours of the morning."

"Not all the time . . . and I don't stay here until the morning all the time, either."

"Who does?"

"We take turns, Frank and I. Sometimes George even takes a turn if things are slow in the mercantile . . . depends."

"Well, it wouldn't be right, just getting a visit from you in the mornings," Millicent continued, shocked. "That just doesn't seem normal. I mean my goodness, how would we ever see each other? Be together? I mean, who would fix you breakfast?"

"Who indeed?" Marshall asked with a secret smile. "We'd have to decide on all of those things, I'm sure."

"And then there's dinner, and lunch, too."

"For a woman who can't cook, you sure are fixated on meals."

She could feel the heat traipse up her neck and over her lace collar. "Well, if I was your wife . . . I'd want to please you."

"You already do," he murmured, taking the quill from her hand and covering her hand with his own. "I don't want to marry you for your dinners."

She grimaced at the statement. Her poor culinary skills were legendary. "I certainly hope not!" Then, because she couldn't resist, she asked, "Why do you?"

His eyes darkened. "Because I want to be able to hold your hand and kiss you anytime I feel like it." He brushed her lips with his own, as if to demonstrate.

"That's why?"

"That's one of the reasons," he said, as he kissed her knuckles. " 'Course, there's others."

"Such as?"

"I want to be near you on a regular basis. I want to look across the room, see a lovely woman in a fancy dress and know that she's my wife. I want to have a feeling of peace inside me that comes from knowing that I am married . . . and am loved."

"Me, too. I want to know I'm loved each day, also."

His expression grew tender. "I don't want you to be alone any longer. I want to have a whole slew of children with you, a whole gaggle of little Millicents, so proper and pretty."

"And boys like you . . . handsome and mischievous."

"Yep," he said expansively, "We'll have a whole slew of them. And we'll raise them right, too. Your parents would be proud."

"And perhaps one day yours will come back from Utah and visit."

"Maybe. If not, we'll write all about them."

"Then we'll have plenty to do."

"Too much. There'll be kids everywhere, needing our attention. Shoot, I bet we're going to miss times like this." He kissed her cheek then, his touch slow and gentle, and oh-so-inviting. She glanced across the room, where Ernestine was chatting with another bargirl that just entered. Neither woman seemed to be paying them the least mind.

Feeling brave, Millicent leaned closer to Marshall . . . so intent on researching this new aspect of their relationship.

"Do you remember the first time I met you, Marshall?" she asked dreamily, tracing a line down his chest with one slim finger.

"I do," he answered, catching her hand and holding it close. "You had on a lavender pinafore and bows in your hair."

She laughed, pleased. "You were catching turtles and tried to give me one."

"It was the best I could do on such short notice." He laughed. "You held it at an arm's length . . . I didn't know if you were admiring it or trying to give it back."

"I didn't want that slimy turtle . . . but I did want to be near you."

"You had the prettiest hair I'd ever seen," he recalled, pulling away, then gazing at her careful chignon. "So filled with flecks of blond and gold, yet so brown and silky. You still do."

"You nodded to my father and told him to watch out for the Indians, though I later found out that there were no unfriendly Indians around here."

"I was trying to impress you. And, I might point out . . . that turtle was not slimy. No turtle is."

She pretended to be miffed. "Oh, how many times have you told me that?"

"Too many to count I imagine," he said, breaking their bond with a small smile. Lazily he leaned back in his chair. "I wonder what your hair would like now, in pigtails?" he asked, returning to their other tangent. "I wonder if it's really as silky and soft as I've always imagined it. Do you brush it a hundred times a night like my mother always did?" he asked softly, his eyes narrowing, as if he was trying to picture her that way. "Do you braid it before sleeping, or does it lay across the pillows, like an invitation to the angels?"

Millicent's eyes widened at his words, his words sounding like poetry to her. She felt that same rush of yearning course through her that she always did, whenever they spoke of private times together. "I, ah . . ."

The speculative gleam in his eye was unnerving. The scene in her mind of them together, with her hair down and his fingers running through it made her throat catch with an unfamiliar and completely unnerving sensation: desire.

"How do you wash it, Millicent? Is it hard to handle by yourself? Have you ever wished for someone to help you? Pour warm water down your back, massage your neck, when it's slick and hot? To wrap it in a cloth and then brush it dry by the fire?" His words were as soft as a caress and his gaze seemed to rest on the small expanse of exposed skin around her neckline.

Millicent touched her chest. Her skin felt heated, flushed. She swallowed hard. "I surely wouldn't know," she said quickly, then picked up her quill again and hurriedly wrote another note.

"Millicent?" he said then, his voice low and husky.

"Yes?"

"Millicent, you know I love you, don't you?"

Her quill dropped in surprise. "Oh . . . Marshall. Really?"

His only answer was a slow grin.

Chapter Twenty-one

At exactly midnight, not four nights after Millicent's kidnapping/rescue, a woman was once again seen traipsing around the town's streets in her nightgown, delivering mail.

Well, actually several women were. They had a mess of letters and were carefully setting them under a whole variety of rocks in town. Each was an invitation to a picnic on Easter Sunday, not one week away.

The moon shone brightly again that night, but not to the extent that it had in the previous week. But bright enough to visibly shine on the faces of the women, should any girl pop her face out of a window and take a look.

'Course, it wouldn't have been the moonlight that would draw a person's attention. Most likely it would be the excited chatter that floated through the air, inviting a person to stare intently at the street . . . to listen hard, on the off chance that a snippet of conversation might be heard.

Miss Millicent slept through the whole thing.

* * *

The next morning came, sure enough, and a steady stream of gentlemen and ladies appeared at George's mercantile, the Dark Horse, the Rocky River bank, and even in the town square, holding neatly folded letters with personal invitations written on them.

Each person was both curious and curiously pleased to be the recipient of such a missive. Gentlemen sat at tables and tried to figure out just who the authors could be, and ladies met at the mercantile to purchase cloth to hurriedly make a new dress for such a party.

Marshall observed it all with a queer sense of fatherly pride. After all, only he could completely understand what the other recipients were going through.

In fact, he realized as he picked up his own note under the infamous gray rock, there was a definite feeling of love in the air.

When he overheard Mrs. Goodwell discussing the finer points of flower bouquets on his walk to work, he knew things were looking up. The courtly nod from Mrs. Thomas only added to his sense of well-being.

Indeed, he was so pleased with the world that he didn't even notice that Edmund Baxter was sitting at the Dark Horse with Justine drinking coffee until he had been there a full ten minutes and had already settled in at a table himself. By that time Marshall figured it was too late to boot Edmund out, especially since Sadie gave him a slight nod of approval and Justine looked so pleased to sit with the older man.

Justine looked completely different than she had only a week ago when she had approached him at the Scarlet. She was devoid of makeup, and wore a plain gray dress. Her hair was pulled severely from her face. But she had a glow about her, one that came from good meals and the knowledge that she was going to be allowed to care for herself, not be told what to do twenty-four hours a day or worry about getting accosted.

Marshall felt happy once again that she'd approached him at the Scarlet Lady. And prouder than ever at Sadie, for it was she who had commandeered Justine and given her the confidence that she so desperately desired.

Then, as if seeing Marshall's attention directed on them, she spoke. "Mr. Bond, would you like us to leave?"

"It's only eleven A.M.," Edmund interrupted gruffly. "She shouldn't be on the clock yet, Bond."

Well, some things never change, Marshall thought to himself. "This is Justine's time . . . her business."

"I was just sitting here, writing a letter home, Boss," Justine said nervously.

"You know I don't care," Marshall replied, then tried to look as interested as he could in the newspaper. But it was hard to ignore the couple's conversation.

"I received a note myself this morning," Edmund said then.

"Did you?" she asked.

"Under a rock, to the left of my favorite wicker chair."

Justine smiled. "I received one, also. A secret one. Do you really think the town can keep such a thing from Miss Millicent?"

"It's worth a try."

"It could work out." Edmund said with a gruff sigh. "Shoot. Strange things are happening in town. Mrs. Thomas didn't even walk to the other side of the street when she saw me coming today," Edmund continued with a wave of his hand. "First, I thought it was because of my new bathing practices, but now I'm not so sure."

Marshall harrumphed to himself.

"Now, I may be mistaken," Justine answered, "but Miss Drovers might have had something to do with that."

"Miss Drovers? Ha! She's been nothing but a bee on my b . . . um, person."

Marshall gripped the table in order not to plant his fist in Baxter's mouth. However, he couldn't help but continue to eavesdrop on one of the most interesting conversations he'd heard in a long time . . . besides his own with Millicent.

"Now you shouldn't say those things about Miss Drovers," Justine said quickly. "I heard that she said you were a true gentleman when she accidentally fell down that shaft during the tour you were giving her of the mine."

Edmund's head popped up. "She said that?"

"She certainly did. And once more, I believe it takes a true gentleman to take charge under that kind of pressure, like you did. You should be proud of yourself."

"Ha," Marshall mumbled.

Edmund threw a scowl his way. "Thank you. That was um . . . kind of Miss Drovers to say those things."

"Miss Drovers is a real lady."

Edmund watched Justine fold her paper neatly and then address the envelope. "So, how'd you end up over here at the Dark Horse, anyway?"

Justine cast a look in Marshall's direction, but he forced himself to keep his head down. "Mr. Bond said I could come on over and try this place out."

"You liking it?"

She nodded. "How could I not? You know how the Scarlet is."

Edmund harrumphed. "I do, at that."

"Well, then you must know how I feel about being able to get on out of there."

Edmund eyed her seriously, seemed to take in every nuance on Justine's face . . . lingering over the faint yellow bruises on her cheek. "What are you going to do now?"

Justine shrugged. "Same as anybody, I reckon. Just live."

"Me, too."

Justine glanced at Marshall, then gazed at Edmund. "I don't know why, but you seem different, somehow."

Edmund grunted. "I'm cleaner."

"That, but changed in other ways, too. Calmer, like you're happy or something."

"Oh, I've just been making some decisions in my life, that's all."

" 'Bout what?"

"Decisions about my future." He propped two fingers in his vest then. "I'll have you know that I've just written away for a genuine mail-order bride."

She looked surprised. "Really? Why you sending off for someone far away?"

"Ladies around here just haven't been too interested in me," Edmund explained. "Figure I'll have a better time bringing someone in."

Her violet eyes flickered to his face, then back at the tabletop. "Perhaps you just haven't been looking around at the right women."

"You think?'

"That's just my opinion, you know."

Edmund leaned back in the chair and folded his hands

over his expanse of belly. "I'll keep that in mind, Justine." He paused for a moment, then continued. "You working a lot?"

"As much as I can. Mr. Bond's pretty strict about my hours, doesn't want me to do a whole lot of overtime . . . he says life's for living, not just for working."

"That right, Bond?" Edmund called out.

Marshall gave up all pretense of pretending not to eavesdrop. He looked over to the couple directly. "Yep."

Edmund scowled, as if he resented having to even speak to him. "So . . . Justine has days off?"

"She does."

Edmund lowered his voice. "You working tonight?"

"Yes."

"You off anytime soon?"

"Tomorrow night."

A slow smile made its way across his face. "That's good to know. I'll keep it in mind."

Not long after that Edmund got up and Marshall strolled over to Justine. "Seems to me like you might have an admirer, there."

Justine blushed. "Oh, Mr. Bond, I don't know."

"To tell you the truth, I've been around Edmund Baxter a lot, and have never seen him linger over coffee before."

She stared at him wistfully, her orchid-colored irises revealing a yearning that was hard not to see. "You'll probably think this sounds funny, but it was kind of nice," she admitted. "I've never had a man just want to sit with me. Usually, he's after something altogether different," she said with a grimace.

Marshall's heart went out to her. Justine looked seventeen if she was a day. It disgusted him that someone so sweet could have been put to work in a place like the Scarlet. "You know, I can't say that I've ever been all that fond of Edmund Baxter . . . but it does look like he's changing. Sometimes it's good to give people the benefit of the doubt."

Justine nodded her head. "I know exactly what you mean."

Marshall patted her hand. "Don't worry about the future. Things will be better from now on, I feel sure of it," he said gently.

"I hope so."

"And Justine, thanks for your help with my picnic project, I don't know what I would have done without y'all the other day."

She smiled at him, the sweet expression lighting up her face. "No problem, Boss. Glad to help."

"Good. Good." Then, catching a glimpse of his timepiece, he sighed. "Speaking of which, I've got about a thousand things to do before the big day. Would you mind helping me a little more? I've decided I ought to make this picnic really special for Millicent, but I'm going to need some help to see my plan through."

"What can I do?"

This time it was Marshall's turn to feel embarrassed. "Justine, I was wondering . . . do you know how to tie bows?"

She blinked. "Bows?"

"George has a whole slew of white ribbon at the mercantile. I was kind of hoping you could help me make some nice bows to decorate the trees and such."

"Decorate the trees for the picnic?"

Marshall fought to keep his expression steady. "I, um,

want to make Sunday as nice as possible for Millicent. She's probably going to remember it for quite a while."

A look of understanding filled Justine's expression. "I'll be happy to make bows for you, Boss. Sunday sounds like it's going to be a grand day."

Marshall smiled broadly. "It surely is."

And then he took off, feeling like things were looking mighty special, indeed. If everybody did their part and kept their mouths shut, there would not only be a beautiful wedding on Sunday, but it would be a surprise for Millicent, too.

He couldn't wait to see her expression when she found out what he'd planned.

Chapter Twenty-two

Word had spread like wildfire through the streets of Rocky River that strange things were afoot. Once it was heard, from mysterious sources, no less, that the picnic was for the whole town—everyone seemed to be shining shoes, brushing their horses to a fine sheen, and baking more pies than you could shake a stick at.

Once more, rumors were abounding that not only was there to be an awfully big picnic, but that a certain famous couple was going to pledge themselves in holy matrimony right before their eyes. Word had also spread that that particular part of the occasion was supposed to be a surprise for the bride-to-be. It became a matter of pride for everyone to keep the secret and plan behind Millicent's back.

Millicent, for her part, knew something was afoot, but couldn't quite place her finger on what it was. Conversations stopped when she entered the mercantile. People cast knowing glances her way when she walked down the street. And Mrs. Anderson sat with her for quite some time on

Saturday morning, just speaking about the benefits of married life.

Even Chrissie had been acting strange. She came over and made a big fuss about what Millicent should wear to the event. When Millicent pulled out a rather plain navy shirtwaist, Chrissie shook her head no and pulled out her pink gown instead.

"You'd look pretty in this on Sunday, Millicent," Chrissie said with a determined look in her eye.

"You don't think it's a little fancy for picnicking?"

"Not at all. I heard most everyone is dressing up special. You need to wear this, and we ought to weave some daisies through your hair, too. It would look so nice."

Millicent shrugged helplessly. "All right, if you think so."

"I know so," Chrissie replied pertly. "Now, in addition, I think we ought to stay inside today and organize your house."

"What? But it's beautiful out! I thought I'd go visit with Mrs. Stover, have a cup of tea with her . . . even try to say hello to Marshall."

Chrissie's eyes widened. "I'm sure that you don't want to see Mrs. Stover today. And George told me that Marshall is busy, too."

Millicent eyed her best friend in speculation. Something was going on, but it was more than obvious that she should stay out of the way. "All right. Let's go get organized," she said, turning with a remarkable lack of enthusiasm to her kitchen shelves.

"Good idea," Chrissie answered, relief evident in her expression.

* * *

For Marshall's part, he had never been so busy in his life. He spent most of the day on Saturday visiting with people and making plans for the wedding. He couldn't believe the amount of details that were involved with such a big undertaking. Thank goodness Chrissie had commandeered Millicent to stay in her home. Not only was he busy with last-minute details, the whole town seemed to have gotten into the nuptial spirit.

He had seen evidence of that late last night when Justine had presented him with an old whiskey carton full of perfect white bows and a big smile.

However, other people had gotten into the act, as well.

Lots of people had begun to help the town's most intriguing couple with their wedding plans, even if nothing was said out loud. Cakes were made, flowers were picked, and one group of ladies even pieced together a large crazy quilt for Millicent to rest on during the festivities.

In addition, gifts, in the form of homemade quilts and linens were collected and cards written. One group of ladies even went so far as to come up with a set of recipes to help Miss Millicent out in her newly married life.

Memories of Saturday night dates and betting pools were conveniently discarded in place of plans for a beautiful wedding and levee afterward. Hurt feelings were exchanged for good wishes, and disappointments led way to speculation over the matrimonial potential of the still-available bachelors.

In fact, Marshall knew that everything was going to be all right when Mrs. Imogene Thomas dared to speak to him the Saturday afternoon before the big day.

"Mr. Bond," she said, as proper as you please.

"Yes, ma'am?"

"I hear there's going to be quite a shindig over in the park tomorrow afternoon."

"Yes ma'am," Marshall said warily, ready for the criticism to let loose.

"I was pleased to receive an invitation, Mr. Bond. I'll look forward to participate in your festivities."

And with that, she walked off, leaving Marshall to stare at her in disbelief.

And finally, all Marshall had left to do was write Millicent an invitation to the festivities and deliver it to her door. He shrugged on his coat at midnight and left his intended her very own love letter.

Dear Millicent,
Would you please do me the honor of being my guest at a four o'clock picnic in the park today? The meal will be good, and the company, I am certain, will be excellent.

Love,
Marshall

Millicent found the note that morning when she opened her door for milk, and tears sprang to her eyes when she read the message. The words, so similar to her own missive, made her smile with delight.

And he'd signed the missive with 'love'.

Marshall loved her.

She knew now that one day they would be together. One day she could plan her wedding and look forward to that day when she'd walk down the aisle to join him in holy matrimony. But until that day came, she would be honored to be courted by him in the open.

And have the bliss of knowing that every Saturday night was his.

So, precisely at 4:00 P.M. sharp, a grand picnic was held in Rocky River's most prominent commons area. The park was so beautiful, Millicent could scarcely believe it. Ribbons and flowers decorated the trees. Someone had strung a few Chinese lanterns along the top of a picnic table.

And more than a hundred people sat on homemade quilts, dressed in their Sunday best, the ladies adorned with new bonnets and parasols. It was a grand occasion, the most remarkable that anyone had seen in some time. Impressive not only for the fancy decorations, but also for the sheer number of guests.

Millicent wore her pink dress, the one that Chrissie had chosen and that Marshall had complimented her on ages ago. The shimmery, dusty rose satin lent an ethereal glow to her skin. The gown was embroidered with flowers and fitted her to perfection.

Because of the day, and knowing Marshall's preference, she wore her hair in a loose chignon as Chrissie had suggested, and threaded some spring daisies through the tresses. She had never felt so grand, or so perfect.

Until she saw that there was a path filled with leaves and flower petals in the middle of it all.

And that the path led right to Preacher Lumkin.

And that Marshall was standing right there beside him. Just as if they were ready for a wedding.

A wedding?

Oh, dear Lord, she was getting married today! Tears sprang to her eyes as she scanned the crowd. Shining expressions returned her gaze. Ladies nodded in agreement.

Men removed their hats. Complete silence reigned for a full two minutes.

Millicent's breath left her. She stood unsteadily in front of them all, trying to unlock her knees. Finally, none other than Justine spoke. "This is all for you, Miss Millicent. So you'd have a big wedding like you and your daddy always dreamed of."

Her throat caught, and for a split second Millicent imagined her father looking down on her from heaven. Looking down on everyone who had helped raise her like they'd promised. She felt the heat from the sun on her shoulders and was sure it was a steady hand from him. Telling her that everything was going to be just fine. She was going to have a wonderful life ahead of her. Tears spilled to her cheeks.

Her daddy would have been touched. He would have been proud . . . of the town, of Marshall, of the men . . . of the woman she had become.

"Go on now, Miss Mill," a gentleman in the back called out. "Time's a'wasting."

"Come on, Miss Millicent, go get married," Anton McKenna said loudly. "It's time now."

Hesitantly, Millicent stepped forward onto the bed of flowers that trailed down among the picnickers. And at the other end of the trail stood Chrissie and George next to Preacher Lumkin, each wearing expressions of pride and love. She met each of the gazes and nodded.

But then she finally caught Marshall's eye. There he stood proudly at the front of the assemblage, looking so handsome and dapper in a suit of gray wool that Millicent had never seen before. A single red rose was pinned to his jacket. His hair looked damp, as if he had just slicked it back from his face. And he wore the most arresting expression Millicent had ever seen. He stared solemnly at her, his eyes shining with love, and admiration, and the promise of a bright future together.

And when the singers from the opera house began to sing "I'll Be True to You," Millicent's eyes pricked with tears and it was all she could do to hold them off. It truly was the happiest day of her life.

Preacher Lumkin officiated wonderfully. He spoke of the generosity of the town, and of the love that filled all of their hearts, and of the steadfast friendship and love that is so necessary for all commitments.

And when he finally said, "I pronounce you man and wife," Millicent could truly feel the approval of her mother and daddy from up in heaven.

"I love you Marshall," she whispered to the man of her dreams. "I always have."

Time seemed to stop. Marshall gazed at her lovingly. A thousand unspoken promises rose between them.

And then Marshall kissed her gently. In the background, George and Chrissie whistled, the roar of the crowd filled her senses, and Millicent knew without a doubt that she and Marshall were going to live happily ever after.

Epilogue

Four weeks had passed since the wedding. Millicent still felt as if she should pinch her cheeks when she awoke each morning over the Dark Horse Saloon. Who would have ever thought that things could have turned out so well?

Here she was, a happily married woman. Chrissie and George were finally engaged, and Marshall seemed to walk around town with a new spring in his step. Things were mighty fine, indeed.

Perhaps it was because summer was finally here, with its bright blue skies and balmy morning air. No longer did Rocky River seemed gripped in spring fever. Life was returning back to normal.

She had even been pleased to hear that Edmund had changed his ways. He was now back to working hard in his mine and squiring girls around town, most especially Justine. Millicent felt certain that one day Edmund and Justine would find true love like she and Marshall had.

In addition, the fathers of Rocky River seemed to hold

Marshall in their favor once again. The grand wedding in the park had moved the town's disposition toward them in a positive way. Everyone now felt as if they'd had a part in the love match, and people had begun inventing parts that they had played in the courtship, even if they'd been out of town for the last few months. Goodness, even the stagecoach drivers had taken to repeating their story to their paying customers.

And now that the men didn't have to worry about their daughters mooning after a saloon owner, they enjoyed partaking their whiskey at the Dark Horse just fine, like they always had. The Dark Horse had even become something of a gentleman's social club instead of just a drinking establishment. Perhaps it was because Ernestine had taken to playing classical music, or maybe it was because everyone knew that Miss Millicent was likely to be up in the living quarters above the bar, and no one dared to offend her sensibilities.

Justine was working out just fine, and Sadie was planning to become a partner in the saloon, with her new pay raise. Business was good.

Millicent was thankful that the betting pool had quietly been torn out of the gaming records. Perhaps one day it would be just a distant memory. That would suit everyone just fine, she imagined.

She was interrupted from her reverie by Marshall's appearance in their bedroom.

"What are you thinking about, sugar?" he asked, after planting a tender kiss on the tip of her nose.

Still shy around her husband, Millicent wrapped her robe a little more snugly around herself as she curled her legs up under her on the couch. "Oh, nothing . . . just how things are working out just fine, after all."

"After all?"

"Well, you know, in spite of the mix-up in letters, and the picnics, and the betting pool."

Marshall pulled out another of his ever-present cheroots and lit it, leaning back in one of the comfortable chairs in their bedroom as he did so. "And the kidnapping, and the threats, and the crazy courtship."

"And the letter writing campaign."

"And the wedding . . ."

She couldn't help but giggle at his description. Truly, put that way, it was amazing that anyone in the town had survived their spring. "Well, it's all behind us, now. And I have a feeling that one day, years from now, we'll not have wanted it any other way."

Marshall seemed to take her words to mind. "I suppose, though I doubt I'll ever forget the feeling that I had when I heard you were down in that mine with Baxter."

"I'll choose to recall that feeling I had when I first saw you on our wedding day."

His lips curved at that. "Or when I first saw you on our wedding night."

She blushed prettily. "What's on your schedule today? I'm going to have tea with Chrissie and meet with Mrs. Anderson about her new fall dresses."

"It doesn't seem to bother Mrs. Anderson that you married me, does it?"

"I should say not."

"Are you sure that you want to still have your business? You're awfully busy now that you are helping me so much around here."

"I don't want to give it up. It gives me something to do when I'm up here by myself at night. Besides, it's a whole different feeling to be making dresses for pin money than when it's out of necessity."

Marshall sighed. "I suppose." He took another puff of his cigar. "Today my schedule is fairly light. I just have to meet with Sadie about a few things and then fill out some invoices for supplies."

"So, does that mean you'd have a few minutes for your wife?"

A wicked gleam entered his eyes. "Depends."

"On what?"

"On what you have in mind."

Feeling brave, Millicent loosened her robe and tried a saucy look over her shoulder as she walked back to bed. "I guess you'll just have to come here and find out," she said with more confidence than she felt.

It must have worked because Marshall put out his cigar and stood up in seconds. "Now that, my dear, is just what I was hoping you'd say."

And then, it was all she could do just to smile. Things were back to normal in Rocky River, Colorado.

Truly, things were far better than that.